PUFFIN BOOKS

RASHA

Muhammed Zafar Iqbal is the best-known writer of science fiction and children's literature from Bangladesh. An educationist, a professor of physics, computer science and engineering, and a social activist—Iqbal is a pioneer in popularizing science and mathematics among the children of Bangladesh. Author of more than 181 books, he is a prolific writer. His books have earned him numerous awards, including the prestigious national Bangla Academy Literary Award.

Arunava Sinha has thirty-five Bengali-to-English published translations in fiction, non-fiction, poetry and children's literature. He is a two-time winner of the Crossword Prize for translated books.

PRAISE FOR THE BOOK

'Incredibly moving story of a young girl whose personal transformation sparks off changes in her surroundings with some amazing results'—Andaleeb Wajid

'A big war, a young country and a little girl who has a big voice and a bigger heart. *Rasha* is not a tale of abandonment, but one of overcoming and prevailing, and the empowerment of young people. A big shout-out to children to say, "If you don't like it, speak up, do something, change wrong to right"'—Paro Anand

LITTLE GIRL, BIG HEART

Muhammed Zafar Iqbal

Translated from the Bengali
by Arunava Sinha

PUFFIN BOOKS

PUFFIN BOOKS

USA | Canada | UK | Ireland | Australia
New Zealand | India | South Africa | China

Puffin Books is part of the Penguin Random House group of companies
whose addresses can be found at global.penguinrandomhouse.com

Published by Penguin Random House India Pvt. Ltd
7th Floor, Infinity Tower C, DLF Cyber City,
Gurgaon 122 002, Haryana, India

First published in Bengali as *Rashed Amar Bondhu* by Tamralipi, Dhaka 2010
First published in Puffin Books by Penguin Random House India 2016

10 9 8 7 6 5 4 3 2

ISBN 9780143434887

Not for sale in Bangladesh

Typeset in Dante MT Std by Manipal Digital Systems, Manipal

Printed at Repro Knowledgecast Limited, India

www.penguin.co.in

In memory of Faraaz Hossain, who died in a terrorist attack in Dhaka because he wouldn't desert his friends

—Arunava Sinha

Contents

Translator's Note

Picture this. Like Marty in *Back to the Future*, you have gone back in time to when your parents were young. Very young. Led by you—or one of your friends—this journey to the past is going to be to the city of Calcutta.

It's 1971.

Schoolchildren in Calcutta are afraid of many things. There's full-blown guerrilla action on the streets, with boys and girls taking up bombs and handmade guns in a bid to usher in a violent leftist revolution.

And barely a few hundred miles away, a country named East Pakistan—the eastern half of Pakistan, which was carved out of undivided India in 1947 by the British rulers before leaving—is fighting a war of independence against West Pakistan. With the Indian Army joining the war against West Pakistan, there are often air-raid sirens and calls for blackouts.

But your parents—and their parents—are not as afraid of these as they are of a mysterious disease that seems to be affecting everyone's eyes. Try telling them that it's only conjunctivitis—an infection that inflames the eyes, which in turn stream continuously. They won't pay attention. Because this affliction has been given a different name, in response to the war of independence being waged by a people with whom most of the inhabitants of Calcutta share a language.

Jai Bangla. Victory to Bangla.

This could variously mean either the region or the language. But it's definitely not meant as a cry of celebration. Thousands of people from East Pakistan are fleeing to India—a second wave, after the first one during the Partition in 1947—and many inhabitants of Calcutta are convinced that *they've* brought the disease over with them.

But once your parents—who were obviously not your parents then—and their parents have explained all this to you, ask them some more questions.

Tell them that you're reading a book about a girl named Rasha from Dhaka, whose grandfather was a freedom fighter in the Bangladesh Liberation War. You will immediately hear your now-grandparents talk of how they—or maybe their closest friends—belonged to families who had actually lived in what is now Bangladesh, having migrated during the Partition of India and the creation of Pakistan.

Ask your parents how they felt about the *Muktijuddho*, the war of liberation, and their response will be—Jai Bangla! And if you see a tear in their eyes, it might not be conjunctivitis alone. It might be the thought of boys and girls their own age across the border, trying to cope with the war and with the loss of their loved ones. Ask them, too, about the *razakars*—the people of East Pakistan who chose not to side with the freedom movement and opted to support the

Pakistan Army and Government instead. You may not get an answer, though. It's hard for young adults to wrap their heads around betrayal.

And you can tell them a few things too—about the novel that you're reading. It's not set in the time of the Muktijuddho, but in the early 2000s. However, it shows us how the large-hearted Rasha is connected to her family's and her country's past—a past that saw an extraordinary struggle being waged for freedom, a past that—it is so feared—many people, both in Bangladesh and India, are beginning to forget.

You can tell them that fourteen-year-old Rasha's parents are divorced and that she lives with her mother, who meets a man whom she wants to marry. That he wants to take Rasha's mother away to Australia, but doesn't want Rasha to join them. And that Rasha's mother decides to leave her daughter with her own mother, who lives in a village.

An unhappy Rasha moves to her grandmother's home, where she discovers a whole new world and a series of adventures. Making friends with a group of boys and girls her own age, and learning from them a novel way of life that involves no modern amenities, such as mobiles, computers, the Internet, movies or even electricity—Rasha plunges into a series of exploits. Thus, she embarks on her own freedom movement—from the tyranny of bad teachers, bad administrators, bad politicians and bad people.

Tell them you wish that they could read this book too.

July 2016 Arunava Sinha

When Abbu and Ammu Turned Weird

When Raisa was ten, a cocky boy in her class had made up a rhyme about her. It began—

> Raisa
> Eats her fish with rice-a

It wasn't funny at all, nor had any of Raisa's classmates paid any attention to the cheeky poet or his creation—but she had burst into tears. Back home she announced that she would change her name. Her mother's eyebrows shot into her hair.

'What do you mean change your name? Do you think a name is like a bedspread that can be changed if you don't like it?'

Instead of getting into an argument with her mother, Raisa calmly proceeded to think up alternative names for herself. She really liked the name Anushka, but since a reckless leap from Raisa to Anushka was ruled out, she chose a name that sounded similar to her own. Dropping the 'i' and adding an 'h', she changed her name to Rasha.

Everyone thought of it as a joke at first, but Raisa did not let up. It didn't happen in a day, or even two, but it was three years later—by the time she was thirteen—that she did, in fact, come to be known as Rasha. Everyone forgot that she had once been called Raisa.

By the time the ten-year-old Raisa had transformed into the thirteen-year-old Rasha, she discovered that the world around her had changed too. At ten she had thought of her parents as the most wonderful people in the world. At thirteen, Rasha discovered that she had been completely mistaken. Her Abbu and Ammu were not nice at all—they had all sorts of problems. Her father was bad-tempered and selfish, caring for nothing but his own interests. Not only that, he lied fluently—even when there was no need to. Gradually Rasha also discovered that her mother was small-minded, an altogether mean kind of woman. She would flare up easily and take to beating the young girl who worked as a domestic help. Rasha felt so ashamed of the two that she wished for the earth to swallow her whole. Slowly things went from bad to worse, and her parents began to have ugly quarrels all the time. At first they would lower their voices so that she couldn't hear them argue, but eventually they stopped caring and began to fight fiercely even in her presence. Their hostility was so awful and their language so atrocious, that Rasha wanted to die.

Then, one day, Rasha's Abbu and Ammu split up. Since Rasha was already aware that something like this was about to happen, she wasn't remotely surprised, although her heart broke with grief. She concluded that her father would move out and, with no one for her mother to quarrel with, there would be some peace at home. Abbu did rent a new house for himself and the arguments died down, but peace did not return. Ammu, who worked in a bank, was fine as long as she was at work but, as soon as she came back home, began to bad-mouth Abbu. And later at night, she whined tearfully. Rasha didn't know what to do. Once or twice she tried to console her mother, but it had just the opposite effect—Ammu blamed Rasha instead, abusing her in the foulest language.

A year passed this way; Rasha turned fourteen. But she felt more like forty. A great deal had happened during this period. Her father had found a middle-aged woman from nowhere, married her and taken off to Canada. Rasha assumed that, with her father out of the country, her mother might *now* calm down and turn her mind to something else.

But that wasn't exactly what happened. Ammu seemed to get even angrier, and the things she said made it seem like it was all Rasha's fault. One day, when Rasha returned from school, she found her mother sitting sullenly in the living room.

'What's the matter, Ammu?' she asked apprehensively.

When her mother didn't answer, Rasha asked again, 'What is it, Ammu?'

Now Ammu exploded with rage, shaking her fist and screaming, 'IS IT ALL MY RESPONSIBILITY? Doesn't your father have any?'

Unable to understand, Rasha asked, 'Responsibility for what?'

'FOR WHAT?' Ammu snarled, her face contorting. 'For you!'

Rasha's heart leapt into her mouth. Wanly she said, 'Responsibility for me?'

'Yes! Are you my daughter alone—or does your father have some duties too? How could he have dumped all the responsibilities on me and escaped to Canada with that canny old woman?'

Rasha felt a stab of fear—as though the ground beneath her feet was shaking. Ammu hadn't said it in as many words yet, but it was obvious what she was *trying* to say. Her father had remarried to start life afresh. But her mother couldn't do it because of *her*.

Rasha's suspicion became firmer with every passing day. Ammu began to take extra care with her appearance before going to work, and started coming home later than usual. Rasha had to frequently eat on her own, with a book for company. She used to be good at her studies, but now she couldn't pay attention to them. She even got two sums wrong in her favourite subject, mathematics!

When returning the answer scripts of an exam, Jahanara Madam, the mathematics teacher, told her, 'Rasha, meet me after class.'

Rasha went to meet her teacher after class, and stood before her with her head bowed.

'What's the matter with you, Rasha?' the teacher asked.

'Nothing, madam,' Rasha answered.

'I'm sure something is. I can see your mind is wandering from your studies. You were *so* good at maths and now you've got not one, but two sums wrong in the exam!'

Rasha was silent.

The teacher said, 'And not just maths—I heard that you've done badly in Bengali too. I can see that you're quiet in class; you don't talk at all. What is it?'

Rasha didn't answer this time either, but tears welled up in her eyes and she bowed her head even lower to hide them.

The teacher said kindly, 'I know your parents are divorced, Rasha. I know that children your age cannot accept it when their parents separate. It creates a crisis, putting pressure on everyone in the family—it must be happening in your case too. But you will have to learn to withstand this kind of pressure. This is quite common nowadays. Sixty per cent of marriages in the Western world end in divorce. We don't have statistics for our country but, if they're checked, the figure will turn out to be close to forty or even fifty per cent! So you will have to accept it.'

'I did accept it, madam,' Rasha finally spoke.

'Well, then?'

'Something else is happening, madam.'

'What else is happening?' Jahanara Madam asked apprehensively.

Rasha couldn't make up her mind whether to tell her teacher or not. She hadn't been able to bare her heart to anyone in a long time. But the kindness in her teacher's voice made her break down today.

Blinking back tears, she said, 'My mother cannot stand me any more, madam.'

The teacher's eyes widened in surprise. 'What are you saying? Your mother can't *stand* you any more! Why not? What have you done?'

'I think Ammu likes someone. She probably wants to marry again.'

Her teacher paused to think before responding. Then she said, 'Look, Rasha, this is quite natural. Your mother's young—how can she spend the rest of her life alone? You must accept this too. In fact, it will probably turn out well for you as well. You'll have someone like a father—a full family with a father *and* a mother. You will enjoy it!'

Rasha shook her head. 'No, madam. That's not what I'm saying.'

'Then what are you saying?'

'My mother cannot get married *because* of me. I am a burden for her. She's wondering how to get rid of me.'

Jahanara Madam was taken aback. After some hesitation, she said, 'Shame on you, Rasha, what *are* you saying? A mother can never think of getting rid of her child!'

Rasha only sighed, without replying.

The teacher said, 'The world survives because of mothers, no mother abandons her child. Do you understand?'

Rasha didn't reply this time either.

Her teacher said, 'I have two children—I'm a mother as well. I *know* these things.'

Rasha was silent still.

The teacher said, 'Don't worry about all this. I'm sure things will be all right. You will have a new family—a complete family. Do you understand what I'm saying?'

Rasha nodded to indicate that she had understood.

As she was about to leave, Jahanara Madam called her back. 'Listen, Rasha. You must come to me whenever you need anything or want to talk about something. All right?'

Rasha nodded again.

Although Jahanara Madam had told Rasha that a mother never deserts her child, Rasha's suspicions turned out to be correct.

One night, when she was working on her computer, Ammu came up to her and said, 'Rasha, what are you doing, my baby?'

Rasha's mother never spoke to her affectionately these days. Even though she was astonished, Rasha didn't let it show. She said, 'I'm trying to check something on the Internet. The Net's so slow . . .'

'I've been thinking of having a chat with you for some time now . . .'

Rasha's heart leapt into her mouth. Forcing herself to stay calm, she asked, 'Yes, Ammu?'

Ammu said, 'You're not a child any more. You're a grown-up girl now, aren't you?'

Not sure of what she should say, Rasha just nodded.

Her mother continued, 'Do you think your father is right in putting the responsibility for you entirely on my shoulders?'

Rasha shook her head tentatively to suggest that it wasn't right.

Looking stern, Ammu said, 'I've tried to take care of you on my own for quite a while. It's time your father took care of you now.'

Rasha looked at her mother, forlorn.

Averting her eyes from her daughter to examine her nail polish with close attention, Ammu declared, 'Call your father. Tell him that he should take you away.'

Rasha didn't know what to say. She spoke after a few attempts, 'W-will Abbu take me?'

'Why not?' Ammu asked harshly. 'Are you my child alone?'

Gulping, Rasha said, 'What if he doesn't?'

Looking at Rasha with slitted eyes, Ammu said, 'If he doesn't, I will have to make *other* arrangements.'

'O-other arrangements? What arrangements?'

'I DON'T KNOW!' Ammu exploded. 'Tell your father to work out whatever arrangements *he* wants!'

Ammu kept sitting there for some more time, delivering a monologue which Rasha heard only partially. She felt as though the world was falling apart, as though all the lights were going out in her room. She felt like she was standing in the middle of an enormous field while a storm was raging in a black sky with a deafening wind and dark clouds everywhere. Rasha could not sleep all night, tossing and turning the hours away.

Two days later, Ammu came up to Rasha again at night, with a cordless telephone in her hand. Holding it out to Rasha, she said, 'Here, call him.'

Rasha knew at once who her mother was referring to. Still she asked, 'Call whom?'

'Your father.'

'Call Abbu? *Now?*'

'Yes.'

Rasha felt helpless. Meekly she said, 'Ammu, *please Ammu . . .*'

'Stop whining! Call him.'

'What should I say?'

'Tell him to take you with him,' said Ammu, her face hard. 'And if not, to make other arrangements for you.'

'Ammu,' Rasha said tearfully, 'you know that I—'

'I don't know anything! I don't want to know either.' Ammu thrust the phone at Rasha's face. 'Call him.'

Regarding her with a long look, Rasha said, 'You really want to get rid of me, Ammu?'

Ammu threw a hissy fit, saying, 'Cut out the drama! *Call him!*'

'What's the number?'

Ammu dialled it herself, listened intently and then handed the phone to Rasha. 'It's ringing.'

Holding the phone to her ear, Rasha heard the other phone ringing, with intervals between rings. After a while there was a click, followed by a deep voice. 'Hello?'

Although Rasha was hearing her father's voice after a long time, she recognized it at once. 'It's Rasha, Abbu,' she said.

Abbu said, 'Excuse me?'

'It's Rasha, Abbu,' she repeated. 'From Bangladesh.'

This time Abbu recognized her voice and seemed to crumble. 'R-Rasha, wh-what news?' he stammered.

'Ammu asked me to call you.'

'Why? What's the matter?'

Rasha didn't exactly know how to tell him. After some hesitation, she finally blurted out breathlessly, 'Ammu-has-asked-you-to-take-me-away!'

'Take you away?' Abbu laughed loudly before continuing. 'Does she think it's so easy? One will need immigration papers, a visa, a plane ticket. Do these things grow on trees?'

Rasha felt even the tips of her ears redden with humiliation. Still she gritted her teeth and said, 'Ammu says she can't look after me any more; you have to do it from now on.'

'Me?' Abbu laughed loudly again, as though what Rasha had said was most amusing. 'How will *I* take responsibility for you? I can barely look after myself! I'm surviving on welfare as an immigrant here. Thankfully it's a civilized nation—else I'd have starved to death!'

Ammu was looking at Rasha with ice-cold eyes. Tearing her eyes away from her mother's, she said, 'You *have* to do something, Abbu. *Please.*'

'What can I do? It's not like I *can* do anything from the other end of the world! She can't just say that she won't look after you. Tell your Ammu to not act crazy.'

Rasha was silent.

Her father said, 'This is how she's always been—no sense of responsibility. What nonsense!'

Rasha didn't respond this time either.

Changing his tone suddenly, Abbu said, 'I'd sent you a card a few days ago—did you get it? A view of Niagara Falls. It's very interesting—half of it is in America and half in Canada. We went to the Canadian side. You wouldn't believe it till you saw it . . .'

Abbu went on talking—telling her over and over again how wonderful a country Canada was, while Bangladesh was lousy. Rasha's mind drifted as he droned on, till she realized that he had disconnected the call.

Holding the phone away from her ear, Rasha looked at her mother.

She asked, 'What's he saying?'

Looking at the floor, Rasha said, 'He says he can't do it.'

'*Can't do it?* The bastard says he can't do it? Didn't he remember what he can and cannot do when having a child?'

Rasha didn't say anything.

Suddenly her mother screamed dementedly, 'Is that bloody father of yours going to be the only one who gets to have fun and travel all around the world, while I sit here in this dirty, dingy lane in Dhaka sucking my thumb? Am I just going to bring up my daughter? Am I not supposed to have any desires of my own?'

Rasha had no idea what to say to this. After a few attempts to speak, she finally said, 'What do you *want*, Ammu? What is it that you want to do?'

'I want to start my life afresh.'

'Do it, Ammu. Do it.'

'Do it?' Ammu screeched. '*How* will I do it? How will I start again while you're hanging around my neck like a millstone? Who can have a new life with a grown-up daughter like you? *How is it possible?*'

Rasha spoke softly, almost inaudibly, 'You can, Ammu—I'm telling you that you can.'

Rasha went to bed very late that night. But first, she researched the various methods of suicide that people resort to around the world. Then, after a very long time, she slept peacefully.

Ammu said nothing to Rasha over the next two weeks, but Rasha knew that something was going on. She didn't know exactly what, but she could guess.

A fortnight later, Ammu came into her room late at night, sat down on her bed and said gently, 'Rasha, there's something I have to tell you, Ma.'

Her tone told Rasha that something big *had* happened. Drawing back from her computer keyboard, she said, 'Yes, Ammu?'

'I'm going away to Australia.'

Rasha didn't understand her, staring at her in surprise. 'Going away where?'

'To Australia.' Ammu took her eyes away from Rasha's and said, 'I know you must be very angry with me, and that's natural. But there was nothing else I could have done!'

'*Australia?*' Rasha muttered again.

'Yes. As you can imagine, no one's going to let me into Australia just like that. So, I've had to marry an Australian citizen. He's a *very* nice man, but—'

Paying no attention, Rasha muttered again, 'Australia . . . Australia . . .'

Ignoring her, Ammu went on, 'He's a good man. Likes me very much but doesn't want any encumbrances. He's not ready to accept my child from a previous marriage.'

Still looking away, Ammu said, 'I'm getting old. Who's going to marry me? This man has agreed, but on one condition. I must leave you behind.'

Rasha's world was destroyed in an instant. She felt a desperate urge to plead, 'Don't go away without me, Ammu!' But she didn't. Instead, she asked, 'Whom will you leave me with?'

'I asked your fupu, but she's your father's sister after all—she didn't agree. Every time I ring her, she disconnects the call.'

Rasha kept looking at her mother.

Ammu muttered, 'I *was* told about a girls' hostel but it's too expensive. *I* can't afford it! It would have been another matter if your father had helped—but he won't!'

Rasha felt a surge of panic.

After a pause, Ammu said, 'I've thought it over and have decided that it's best to send you to your nani. Your grandmother will look after you. She'll be good to you.'

Unable to believe her ears, Rasha stared at her mother open-mouthed.

Ammu said, 'I see no other option besides your nani.'

Making an effort to speak, Rasha said, 'But Nani's mad, Ammu.'

Ammu tried to laugh it off. 'She *is* a bit eccentric, but then, who isn't? A shock like that at such a young age would make anyone go mad.'

'*You* never go to Nani's house. You've never let me go either. You've always said that she's stark raving mad, that she should be kept tied up. You said . . .'

Ammu said, 'But who else can I leave you with? Besides, I've heard she's much better now. She's managing the house, isn't she? How could she have done it if she were crazy?'

'What about school?'

At this Ammu looked startled. Fumbling for words, she said, 'Th-there m-must be a school in the village. You can attend that. You don't get an education at school, after all, you educate yourself!'

Rasha hid her face in her hands.

Ammu whispered, 'Give me a little time, Ma. Let me settle down in Australia, I'll take you afterwards. *I promise.*'

Rasha didn't say a word.

Ammu said, 'Don't be angry with me, Ma. I had no choice. Believe me, I didn't. Can a mother ever leave her child behind if she can help it?'

Then Ammu began to sob loudly. Rasha looked at her mother, but she saw nothing. She was thinking of the methods of suicide that she had looked up on the Internet. Several had been mentioned—but now she couldn't remember a single one.

Not a single one. Not that it mattered right now, because she would only have to remember one when the time came. And she was certain that she would recollect it then.

A Remote Village

Stopping his rickshaw-van by the side of the road, the rickshaw driver wiped his face with a *gamchha* and said, 'Can't go any further. You'll have to walk the rest of the way.'

'Walk the rest of the way?' Ammu repeated distractedly.

'Yes.' The middle-aged rickshaw driver pointed to the unpaved road. 'This road is completely flooded during the rains. You have to take a boat then.'

'I see,' said Ammu. She was back here after a very long time. These days she no longer recognized a place that she hadn't visited in some time. What used to be open spaces were now congested with buildings and people. But this area hadn't seen much change; it was the same as she had seen it as a child.

Rasha had drawn her feet up on to the rickshaw-van. She jumped off. They had left the city last evening, travelling overnight by train and taking a bus in the morning. After the bus, a scooter, and then, finally, this rickshaw-van. Now they would have to walk the rest of the way. Rasha looked around absently, but didn't seem to notice anything. A kingfisher had been sitting on a tree by a pond a little while ago. She had never seen a bird as beautiful and iridescent—but still she felt no joy at the sight. She seemed to have died a little inside, feeling neither happiness nor sorrow any more. What was happening around her was nothing but a nightmare. Sometimes she felt that she would wake up any moment and find herself sitting in front of her computer in her room back home. But Rasha knew that this wasn't a nightmare but a reality, which was why her heart was numb with a completely unfamiliar despair, sadness and fear.

Getting off the rickshaw-van, Ammu said, 'We have to walk now, Ma. You *can* do it, can't you?'

Rasha nodded without a word to indicate that she could. The rickshaw driver pulled Ammu's bag and Rasha's large suitcase off the van. All that she would need to spend the rest of her life had been stuffed into the suitcase. Her mother had told her repeatedly, 'Take all you need, Ma. You won't have another chance.' Rasha hadn't given it much thought, listlessly packing whatever was at hand into her suitcase. She still couldn't believe that it was really happening.

She had some clothes in the suitcase and some books too. She would have liked to have brought her computer along, but Ammu had told her that there was no electricity where they were going. And besides, how would she have brought something as large as a computer? The suitcase had proved difficult enough.

Her suitcase had wheels and, had the road been a good one, she could have wheeled it along. But she had no idea how to carry it across this muddy, unpaved road.

Ammu told the rickshaw driver, 'I'll be going back today—I'm not staying the night. Don't forget.'

'I won't,' he said.

Pointing to Rasha's suitcase, Ammu said, 'This suitcase has to be taken where we're going. Is there anyone to help us with it?'

'I'll take it,' the man offered.

'What about your rickshaw? What if someone makes off with it?'

'I'll leave it at someone's house here. No one will make off with it. We all know one another in this village.'

Soon the small party of three were on their way, led by the rickshaw driver carrying Rasha's suitcase on his head, followed by Ammu and then by Rasha. Ammu tried to talk to Rasha at intervals but Rasha gave monosyllabic replies, so the conversation petered out.

Rasha looked around her as they walked along the village road. If her classmates had come here for a picnic—the farmland, the fields, the canals, the trees, the cows, the goats, the birds and so on would have surely excited them. They would have run about in the fields, dived into the canal, taken pictures with the cattle. But that scenario seemed utterly meaningless to her now. There weren't too many people on the road, just one or two now and then. They turned around to look at Rasha and her mother curiously. Rasha examined one of them closely—a frail girl of eight or nine, her skin darkened by the sun, her unkempt hair reddened by grime and flying in the wind, bare-bodied and dressed only in a pair of oversized shorts. She was holding a strip of bamboo, using it disinterestedly to guide an enormous bull. Rasha's heart quaked at its sharp horns and cruel red eyes, but the slender young girl seemed fearless. Rasha stared at her in surprise.

Pausing under a large banyan tree, Ammu said, 'See that palm tree? That's where your nani lives.' Rasha was silent. 'There used to be two trees there but one of them was struck by lightning,' her mother told her.

Rasha didn't respond this time either, trying to picture two palm trees instead of one.

The road narrowed even more, leading to a ramshackle bamboo bridge. Ammu crossed it with her sandals in her hand, while Rasha walked across without taking her shoes off. Then they passed a cluster of wild bushes and thickets of trees. Finally, Ammu stopped in front of a faded tin structure. 'This is your Nani's house,' she said.

Rasha looked up. She had seen images of houses like these when news from the villages came on television, but this was her first real one. Ammu walked past the outer room into a yard, with two rooms on either side. One had a tin roof and the other, a thatched one. The huge yard was spanking clean. Not a soul was to be seen anywhere—only a hen could be spotted, strutting around with her chicks and pecking food off the ground. The hen clucked a sound of caution when she saw them, whereupon her children rushed to take shelter under her wing. Once they realized there was no danger, they dispersed again.

Lowering the suitcase to the ground, the rickshaw driver wiped his face and neck with his gamchha again. Ammu looked around and then said loudly, 'Ma!'

No one responded. Ammu knocked on the door of one of the rooms, which opened immediately at her touch. She went in, emerging a little later to announce, 'There's no one in there.'

Rasha said nothing.

'Let's go around the back,' said Ammu. 'Maybe she's at the pond.'

Ammu set off past the tin rooms for the rear of the house. Unable to decide whether to wait or to follow, Rasha eventually trailed along. There were large trees and bamboo groves at the back, and Rasha passed beneath them, dry leaves crunching under her feet. A large pond lay ahead, brimming with dark water. A ghat lay in the shade, the steps leading down. Rasha saw a woman on the steps, sitting with her back to them, so that her face wasn't visible.

'Ma,' said Ammu.

'Who is it?' the woman asked without turning her head.

'It's me, Ma. Nilu.'

Nilu was Rasha's mother's nickname, but no one had addressed her by that name in a long time.

Without a single backward glance, the woman on the steps asked, 'Who's that with you?'

'My daughter, Rasha.'

Ammu went down the steps to stand next to her mother, who still made no attempt to look at her.

Coldly she asked, 'And why are you visiting your mad mother?'

Ammu was taken aback. 'No, I mean . . .' she stammered.

'You haven't asked after me even once in all these years. And now you're here with your daughter! What's going on?'

Hesitating, Ammu said, 'Actually I'm going abroad—to Australia. And I can't take Rasha with me. So I thought I'd leave her here with you.'

'How long are you going away for?'

'Um . . . actually, for quite some time. The thing is—'

'Are you marrying someone else?'

Ammu's face was drained of colour. Lowering her eyes, she said, 'Yes.'

'Your new husband won't accept your daughter?'

Ammu was silent.

'And so you're dumping her here? Why didn't you just slit her throat and let her body drift away in the river? How will your daughter live in a village?'

'You don't understand, Ma,' Ammu protested. 'I had no choice—'

'It's true—I'm scatterbrained. It's also true that I'm mad. But I'm not a fool, Nilu! Why are you ruining your daughter's life?'

'I'm not ruining her life Ma . . . once I've settled down—'

Rasha saw Nani raising her arm to cut her mother short. 'Where's my granddaughter? Let me see my poor girl.'

Finally Rasha's grandmother turned around, slowly—giving Rasha her first glimpse of her mad granny. Over the past few days, she had often tried to imagine what her nani might look like. Coarse strands of white hair, sunken cheeks, hundreds of wrinkles and angry red eyes were what came to her mind—but to Rasha's utter surprise, she realized that her grandmother's face showed no signs of ageing. She looked as if she were Rasha's mother's elder sister! Her hair *had* greyed a little, she was sunburnt and her eyes shone brightly. Rasha felt those eyes probing her.

Nani gazed at Rasha intently for some time before waving her closer. 'Come to me,' she said.

Rasha walked up to her in trepidation. Nani took her hand, drew her close and whispered, 'I *knew* you'd come. That's why I was waiting, all dressed up.'

'What did you say?' Rasha looked at her grandmother in surprise.

'I said I was waiting for you. I knew you'd come today.'

'How did you know?'

'I'm a mad woman, you see—I have strange notions. This morning I was convinced that you would be coming. That's why I took this sari out of the trunk and put it on!'

Rasha stared disbelievingly at her mad grandmother.

Summoning a smile to her face, Nani said, 'You don't believe me, do you? All right, give me your hand.'

Rasha did. Her grandmother unclenched her fist and transferred something from it, closing Rasha's fingers around it, 'Here, I've been waiting to give this to you. It's yours now.'

'What is it?'

'My mother gave it to me. She got it from her mother, who got it from her mother . . .'

'*What is it?*' Rasha asked again, curious now.

'An amulet.'

'What does it do?'

'Come closer, let me whisper in your ear.'

Rasha leaned forward. Her grandmother held her chin, brought her mouth to Rasha's ear and said, 'When your heart is pure, any wish you make with this will come true.'

'*Any* wish?'

'Yes, but you mustn't ask for just anything you want. Mustn't wish for things that are impossible. If you do that, the amulet loses its power. It's lost its power for me. My wishes don't come true any more. But yours will.'

'How did you make it lose its power?'

'I asked for Nilu's father to be alive again. And its power was lost. You mustn't ask for someone to be brought back to life after death—'

'Why are you telling Rasha all this, Ma?' interrupted Ammu.

'Because I *want* to,' Nani answered. 'What business is it of yours? Why are *you* abandoning your daughter with me? Did I ask you to?'

'No . . . what I meant is, Rasha is a child. If she starts believing in all this . . .'

'Why shouldn't she? Am I lying?'

Ammu lapsed into silence.

Pulling Rasha's head close again, Nani whispered, 'I didn't give your mother this amulet. I kept it for *you*.'

'Why?'

Lowering her voice so that Ammu couldn't hear, Nani said, 'She isn't worthy of it. *You* have to be worthy.'

'And I'm worthy?'

'You are.'

Rasha looked into Nani's eyes. She smiled, her stern face softening suddenly.

Clutching the amulet tightly, Rasha said, 'Protect me, Lord, *please*—I'm in deep trouble.'

Taking Rasha's hand in a corner of the yard, her mother burst into tears. 'Forgive me, Rasha Ma.'

Rasha did not speak.

Ammu said, 'I think Ma was right—it would have been better to have slit your throat and cast you in the river!'

Rasha didn't speak this time either.

Still sobbing, Ammu promised, 'I'll fetch you as soon as I've settled down. I swear on the Lord!'

Blinking back her own tears now, Rasha said, 'All right.'

Pulling a thick envelope out of her bag, Ammu handed it to Rasha. 'Keep this.'

'What is it?'

'Some money. I couldn't put in much. Ten thousand taka. Keep it hidden, don't let anyone know.'

'What will I do with money?' asked Rasha.

'You'll need it. Take it, Ma.'

Rasha accepted the envelope.

Wiping her eyes, Ammu said, 'Listen.'

'What?'

'Don't believe all the strange things your nani says. She's mad, she says a lot of funny things.'

Rasha did not respond but Ammu explained, 'She slowly went mad after they killed Baba in 1971.'

'I see,' said Rasha.

'She *is* mad, but you must bear with her.'

'I will.'

Ammu put her arms around Rasha, holding her for a while. Then she looked at her daughter and said, 'I'll go now.'

'All right.'

'Say something.'

'Say what?'

'Don't you want to tell your mother *anything*?'

'Don't worry about me. I'll look after myself, Ammu.'

Rasha found herself smiling against her wishes. But there was no joy in the smile, only a deep sadness. Ammu looked at her in surprise, and then turned around to walk off.

Rasha sat in the veranda of the tin house, looking at her mother's retreating back. The hen was still clucking about with her chicks. The little birds stayed near their mother, secure and protected from danger. Meanwhile, Rasha watched her own mother leave after abandoning her with her mad grandmother in a remote village.

She covered her face with her hands, muttering, 'I won't cry, I won't cry—*no way am I going to cry!*'

Still she burst into tears.

Mad Nani

Rasha was sitting cross-legged in the veranda, surrounded by a small crowd. Several children with protruding bellies were staring at her inquisitively. They didn't have a stitch on them—the only 'garment' being a black thread wound around their waists, from which hung a number of amulets in different shapes and sizes. There were a few young girls too, one or two of them in saris, which made them look positively grown up. Some sickly looking women were present as well, with limp babies in their arms. All the babies wore amulets too, around their necks.

Rasha wasn't sure what she should do. The people clustered around were just staring at her in silence, without saying a word. She was wondering whether to ask them what they wanted when one of the women asked, 'Aren't you Nilu Bubu's daughter?'

Rasha nodded.

Now the woman said, 'Your father has left your mother, hasn't he?'

Rasha looked at her in mild surprise. All her classmates had come to know of her parents separating, but not even once had any of them asked her about it. And here a complete stranger was asking her about it with such ease. Before she could answer, another woman said, 'We *know* he has.'

'How do you and your mother manage?' the first woman inquired.

Rasha couldn't believe her own ears! How could anyone ask such questions? When she continued to look at the woman in astonishment, yet another one said, 'They must be running short of money. Why else would Nilu Bubu have left her daughter *here*?'

'It's very hard when your husband leaves you,' a young woman said gravely.

An older woman said to the others, 'Don't you remember Jamila? She'd had to go to her father with her two children. He had been starving already, and then he'd had to feed his daughter *and* her two children!'

Rasha was listening to the conversation with bated breath when a girl of seven or eight asked her, 'What's your name?'

'Rasha.'

'*Rasha?* What kind of name is *that*?'

'What's wrong with it?'

'We've never heard of a name like this.'

A middle-aged woman said, 'That's the kind of name city people have! My sister-in-law has named her children that way—Turka, Murka . . .'

The children laughed in delight on hearing that this was how city people named their sons and daughters. A boy with a dripping nose mustered up the courage to step up, trying to touch Rasha on her elbow.

The woman asked, 'Are you married?'

'*Married?* Me?' Rasha's eyebrows shot up.

'Yes.'

'Why should I be married so soon? I'm only in class eight!'

The woman whose sister-in-law's children were named Turka and Murka said in all seriousness, 'City girls get married very late . . .'

A young girl, who looked older than her age because she was dressed in a sari, asked, 'How long will you stay here?'

Trying hard to look nonchalant, Rasha answered, 'I don't know—I think I'll be here for a while.'

The conversation would have continued had Nani not materialized suddenly. The naked little children ran away in fear as soon as they saw her; the older boys, the girls as well as the women retreated a few steps too.

Narrowing her eyes, Nani asked everyone, 'What are you here for—is this a circus?'

A middle-aged woman replied, 'No, Fupu. We heard that Nilu Bubu's daughter was here, so—'

'If it *isn't* a circus, what's the big crowd for? Go home, all of you!'

They left without a word.

Stepping out of the veranda, Rasha said, 'Thank you, Nani.'

'You'll have to bear it for a while,' Nani said. 'There's nothing for anyone to do in these villages—even the birth of a baby goat is a big event. People from a dozen villages gather to see it. And you're a fully fledged human being! How can you expect them not to gape at you?'

Rasha did not reply. Her grandmother disappeared inside the house, still talking to herself, and Rasha remained standing in the middle of the yard. Nani was probably right, she concluded. In a place where nothing *ever* happened, the arrival of a young girl from the city, whose parents had separated, was obviously big news. It was quite natural for the villagers to want a glimpse of her. But Rasha wished that she could hide somewhere. She also had no idea which part of the house she would live in. Let alone hiding somewhere, she didn't even know whether she'd have some space of her own.

The pond at the back of the house was secluded. Hoping that no one would turn up there without warning, Rasha went in that direction. Sitting on the steps that lead down to the water would make her visible to everyone. So she went further down, to find a spot hidden to the eye.

Gazing at the still water, Rasha realized that it was, in fact, a very beautiful place. But since she had been down in the dumps, she hadn't noticed the trees and the birdsong.

It was a desolate spot, a little eerie even. She sat in silence, leaning back against the steps. She hadn't entirely grasped the situation yet, unable to accept the fact that she might well have to spend the rest of her life here. She didn't yet know whether she would have the chance to continue her studies. Rasha felt like she couldn't breathe.

That's when she heard footsteps. Someone was approaching. Soon she saw who it was—a scrawny boy of seven or eight with unkempt hair and a grimy body. He was singing to himself utterly tunelessly—a fact that didn't seem to bother him at all. Because Rasha was sitting where she wouldn't be visible, the boy didn't see her. Stopping at the edge of the water, he took off his shirt, flinging it away, and proceeded to take his shorts off as well.

Just then Rasha cleared her throat so that he wouldn't be embarrassed at having been caught with his pants down in the presence of a girl. But the reaction was violent. The emaciated little boy turned around, startled, and emitted a terrified scream on catching sight of Rasha. And before she knew what was going on, he lost his balance and fell into the water with a loud splash.

Rasha stood up in confusion. By then the boy had swum to the middle of the pond, from where he began to shriek again.

'What is it?' asked Rasha. 'What's the matter with you?'

Swimming to the opposite bank, the boy yelled, 'A ghost!'

'*A ghost?*' Rasha was baffled. 'What ghost?'

'You!'

'*Me?*' asked Rasha in consternation. 'I'm a ghost?'

'Yes!'

'No,' she shook her head. 'I'm not a ghost.'

'You swear on the Lord?'

'I swear on the Lord.'

'Then who are you?'

'This is my nani's house. I've come to stay with her. My name is Rasha.'

'Lasha?'

'Not Lasha, Rasha.'

The boy must have been a water-fly. Floating on the water, he said, 'You aren't lying?'

'No, it's the truth.'

Finally he swam towards Rasha. Standing on the moss-covered steps, he looked doubtfully at her. Water dripped from his hair. When Rasha made to take a step towards him, he shouted, 'Don't come near me!'

Rasha stopped. 'All right, I won't.'

'This is your nani's house?' he asked.

'Yes.'

'You're lying!'

'Why should I be lying?'

'Because I've never seen you here before.'

'I've never *been* here before, that's why.'

'You swear on the Lord?'

'I swear on the Lord,' said Rasha.

The boy appeared to believe her at last. Climbing up the steps, he said, 'I got *so* scared when I saw you!'

'*Scared?* Why?'

'Tuesday afternoons are ominous. That's when the spirits come out.'

Rasha chuckled. To tell the truth, this was the first time in ages that she had laughed.

Flying into a rage at this, the boy asked hotly, 'Why do you laugh? What are you laughing at?'

'At what you said.'

'What did I say that's so funny?'

'That thing about spirits.'

'Are you trying to tell me that spirits *don't* come out on Tuesdays and Saturdays?'

'If spirits existed, they wouldn't wait for Tuesdays and Saturdays. They would come out every day. There's no such thing as spirits.'

The boy stared at Rasha sceptically. He looked distinctly offended at what she had said. Angrily he said, 'It's not right to talk of things you know nothing about!'

'I *do* know. That's why I said what I did.'

'You don't believe in jinns and ghosts and spirits?'

'No.'

'You'll see what happens when you do see one!'

Smiling, Rasha asked, 'Can you show me a ghost?'

'That's easy. Just go to the graveyard on a dark night, when the moon's not out, and you'll find ghouls *and* banshees roaming around.'

Widening her smile, Rasha said, 'Can you get hold of a ghost for me?'

'Get hold of a ghost?'

'Yes. If you can get me a ghost, I'll give you 100 taka. And if you can put it in a bottle, 130!'

The boy looked at Rasha for a few moments before asking, 'Are you joking with me?'

'Yes,' Rasha nodded.

He should have become angrier still, but he suddenly grinned. 'You're very stranger,' he said.

'*Strange*, not stranger. Stranger means something else.'

Laughing loudly now, the boy said, 'Stranger, stranger, completely stranger!'

'What's your name?' Rasha asked him.

'Jitu. Jitu Mian.'

'Very good, Jitu Mian! Now we've met.'

About to plunge into the water again, Jitu Mian stopped. 'What should I call you?' he asked. 'Should I call you Rasha Fupu?'

'Don't you dare! I'll kill you if you address me as Fupu.'

'But that's the relationship. Your mother is my grandmother's cousin—'

'I don't understand all this. But you mustn't call me Fupu. I'll kill you if you do!'

Jitu Mian was delighted at this. Laughing with all his teeth on display, he sang, 'Stranger, stranger. You're completely stranger!'

'If I 'm stranger, then so be it.'

'What should I call you then?'

'My name is Rasha. Call me Rasha.'

Jitu Mian bit his tongue. 'Impossible! You're older than me—it's a sin to call you by your name.'

'Then try Rasha Apu? "Rashapu" for short.'

This name Jitu Mian loved. Giggling, he said, 'Rashapu! *Ra-sha-pu!* This is perfect. People will probably say I'm mad to address my fupu as Apu. But let them.'

Jitu Mian leapt into the water from where he was, disappearing under the surface. He wasn't to be seen for some time. Then he suddenly popped up in the middle of the pond, shouted a few words, and vanished again. Rasha was very envious at the ease with which he was playing in the water—he seemed-better suited to the water than to land. If only she knew how to swim, just like this boy, she would have jumped in too.

Evening came in an unusual way to Nani's house. Everyone around seemed to have realized that the sun would set soon, and that they should return home. The cows came back in single file. The ducks waddled out of the water. Even the cocks and hens entered their coops busily. The sound of birds calling in the trees grew a hundred times louder, and large bats began to take flight. The sound of conch shells was heard from a distance, followed by the azan. Then darkness descended everywhere. Since there was no electricity, no lights came on. Nani lit a hurricane lantern and two small lamps. The flame of the lamp flickered like a living thing, and Rasha gazed in surprise at the large, wriggling shadow it threw on the wall. Rasha had never seen total darkness before this. Back home, whenever the room would go dark, she would quickly switch on the light, dispelling the darkness at once. For the first time she felt darkness closing in on her—the two lamps were unable to keep it away. On the contrary, their feeble light made the darkness seem even heavier.

Rasha sat in silence in the veranda. She listened to the chirping of the birds die down. Only a faint rustling of the leaves could be heard. It was an eerie sound, making the heart bereft.

Suddenly, there was a *whoa-whoa-whoa* sort of sound in a human voice, somewhere very close by. Rasha was startled, her heart hammering with fear. She leapt up and ran inside. Nani was cooking on a clay oven in a corner of the kitchen.

'What's the matter?' Nani asked when she saw Rasha run in.

'What's that noise?'

'What noise?' asked Nani.

'That cry!'

Nani listened closely and then chuckled. 'Haven't you ever heard a fox before?'

'That's a *fox*?'

'Yes.'

'How strange—*just* like a human voice.'

'Who knows, maybe it is one! Foxes steal human babies sometimes, and bring them up as their own.'

'*Really?*'

'Yes. The foxes here were a menace when I was young. Then everyone smoked them out of their holes and beat them to death. Once, when they were getting rid of a dead fox, they found one that looked different—no tail, no fur. When they examined it carefully, they discovered that it was a human baby.'

Rasha shivered. 'Poor thing . . .'

'You have to be careful when you have a baby in the village.'

Nani added some dry leaves to the oven to stoke the fire. She was sitting very close to the hot flames, but it didn't seem to bother her. Rasha watched her cook for a while before returning to her spot in the veranda.

Once her eyes had readjusted to the darkness, she could see things dimly. Glancing at the sky, Rasha was astonished. Millions of stars seemed to be twinkling up there. She had never realized that there were so many stars in the sky! To tell the truth, she had never even looked at the sky properly. She couldn't have imagined how beautiful the sight of shining stars could be. At that moment, she saw one shooting across—how amazing! She had read about meteors that burnt themselves out as they blazed across space, but she was seeing one for the first time. Rasha stared at the night sky, mesmerized.

The dinner arrangements were frugal. A sheet had been laid out on the floor, and plates and the pot of food were placed on it. Nani sat down on a low wooden stool, her legs stretched out, and put her plate on her lap.

Serving Rasha, she said, 'I don't know if you'll enjoy this. *I* used to eat anything I could get my hands on—but you can't do that.'

'If you could, so can I,' said Rasha.

Nani shook her head. 'No. You're a growing child. You must eat well.'

Nani piled food on Rasha's plate. Rice, vegetables, chicken curry. Rasha was ravenous; she gobbled it all down like a demon. It was a little spicy, but delicious—completely different from the food she got at home, which would be taken out of a fridge and reheated. Here, everything smelled fresh.

'You cook so well, Nani!' said Rasha.

Nani smiled. 'I could, once upon a time. I've lost the habit. You can't cook for yourself—you must have someone else to cook for. Your nana was very fond of good food . . .'

Nani suddenly looked distracted. She sat in silence, her plate on her lap. There was a strangely vacant look in her eyes. About to speak, Rasha stopped.

Nani was scaring her.

Rasha had been worried about the sleeping arrangements because there was just one small bed in the room.

Soon after they had eaten, Nani spread a clean sheet on it and said, 'Go to sleep now.'

'What about you?' Rasha asked.

'I'll spread a mat on the floor.'

'Impossible! You must sleep on the bed, Nani. I'll sleep on the floor.'

'You'll sleep on the floor?'

'Yes.'

'You won't be scared when a rat scampers over you at night, will you?'

'*A rat?*' Rasha eyebrows shot up. 'Over me!'

Nani smiled. 'I'm joking, you silly girl! Of course there are rats, but they aren't stupid enough to scurry about around humans.'

'R-really? There *are* rats here?'

'Naturally, it's a village after all. But the rats mind their own business, and we mind ours. We don't get in each other's way.'

'But that doesn't mean the rats—'

'If you're terrified of rats, what will you do when you see a snake?'

'There are snakes too?' Rasha turned pale. '*In* the house?'

'Not now. But when it rains, they do enter the house sometimes. Snakes also have to take shelter somewhere, after all.'

'Don't they bite?'

'Why would they bite without provocation? We don't bother them and they don't bother us.'

Rasha hesitated. 'Nani . . .?'

'What now?'

'I have an idea.'

'What's that?'

'You come up on the bed too. There's room for both of us.'

Nani smiled. 'You won't be able to sleep if I do. I can't sleep all night. All I do is toss and turn. I'm mad, you see—my head's messed up. I see strange sights. I moan, I sigh. Actually, I spend most nights in the veranda.'

'What do you do in the veranda?'

'Nothing. I just try to calm myself down.'

'OK,' said Rasha, not sure how to respond. A little later she said, 'I was sitting in the veranda too, looking at the stars.'

Nani nodded. 'Millions of stars up there.'

'I saw one streak across the sky and disappear. I think it fell.'

'What did you wish for?'

'*Wish?* What do you mean?'

'Don't you know? If you make a wish when a star shoots across the sky, whatever you wish for comes true.'

'Really?'

'That's what people say. You can try next time.'

Rasha went to bed when the darkness had deepened, but she was astonished when she looked at her watch. It was only 9.30 p.m., though it felt like much later in the night.

In bed, Rasha moved around restlessly. The day had passed somehow but, now, lying on a soft sheet on a tiny bed in a dark room, Rasha felt her heart breaking into pieces. She used to study at a wonderful school, with friends she loved, and was the apple of her teachers' eyes. Yes, her father had left and she had grown distant from her mother. But still, she had her own room and, in it, her favourite books. It was true that the sky couldn't be seen from the window but the road was visible and, on it, pedestrians and cars and buses. Her computer was her companion and it was a sort of window too, through which she could peep at the entire world. Now she was stuck here in a small tin house with her deranged grandmother. No studies, no school and the village people staring at her constantly. Day after day, month after month, year after year. How would she live here all by herself? Wouldn't it have been better to die?

Now Rasha couldn't restrain herself any more, bursting into tears. She tried her utmost to control herself but it was useless. Her body was wracked with sobs.

Suddenly Rasha felt the touch of a hand on her forehead. Her grandmother was sitting by her, stroking her brow. Rasha heard Nani whisper, 'Don't cry, *shona*. I don't know what to do when someone cries.'

Turning towards Nani, Rasha put her head on her lap and wept helplessly. 'What'll happen to me, Nani? What'll happen to me now?'

'Everything will be all right, shona. You'll see.'

'*How* will it be all right, Nani? I wanted to study. I used to go to such a wonderful school, I had friends, I had teachers. What will I do here alone? How will I manage?'

'Everything will be all right, shona.'

'No it won't, Nani. It won't,' Rasha said through her tears. 'I know it won't. I'll die, Nani, I'll die!'

Nani caressed her granddaughter's face. 'No, shona, you mustn't say that. I'm a mad woman; there are many things I don't understand. But there's one thing that I do understand—that you must live. When you die, everything ends—there's nothing you can do after that. But while you're alive, you can find a way. Everything will turn out all right, you'll see.'

'Are you sure, Nani?'

'Yes, shona. I'm sure.'

Rasha sobbed uncontrollably, clinging tightly to Nani. She didn't even know this person twenty-four hours ago, she had never seen her. And now this mad grandmother was Rasha's only source of security.

Nani ran her fingers through her granddaughter's hair. Rasha felt bewildered by the confusing thoughts racing through her head. But Nani held her close.

Getting to Know Everyone

Rasha woke up early; it wasn't even dawn yet. From her bed she could hear Nani sweeping the yard. Rasha had no idea why this had to be done so early in the day. Getting out of bed, she opened the door and went out to the veranda.

Nani stopped sweeping when she saw Rasha and stood upright. 'Why are you up so early?'

'I woke up. Why are you sweeping the yard at this hour?'

'I don't know.'

'You don't know?'

'No. I have to pass the time somehow, so I work.'

'Give me the broom. Let me do it.'

Nani smiled. 'You don't have to sweep the yard.'

'I can do it, Nani.'

'I know you can—it's not particularly difficult.'

'Then why not?'

'I'm not all right in the head, so *I* do strange things. Why should *you*?'

Rasha stepped into the yard. 'What should I do then?'

'If you must do something, go open the doors to the hen coop.'

As soon as Rasha opened the door of the coop, in one corner of the yard, the cock and hen came out crowing, followed by the waddling ducks. The hen fluttered her wings noisily, whereupon her squealing chicks surrounded her. Such a lovely sight!

'Check for eggs inside,' said Nani.

Bending down and peering in, Rasha discovered that there were indeed two eggs. Bringing them out, she exclaimed, 'So amazing!'

'What's amazing?'

'These eggs here. I'm just so used to finding eggs in the fridge. I'd completely forgotten that they actually come from hens and ducks!'

'Go brush your teeth. I'll make you eggs for breakfast.'

A little later, the women and girls of the village began to appear, intent on catching a glimpse of Rasha again. There was great curiosity about the girl whose parents had separated and whose mother had left her with her mad grandmother in the village. Rasha sat stiffly for a while, but soon the whole thing became unbearable. She went into the room on the pretext of a headache and wrapped herself in a sheet on the bed.

When the disappointed women had left, Nani sat down next to Rasha, putting her hand on her brow and asking, 'Are you feeling very ill?'

Rasha sat up. 'No, Nani. I'm fine. It's just that I can't stand all these people coming here to see me.'

'I see,' said Nani.

'Am I a strange beast for everyone to gape at?'

Nani smiled. 'Actually you *are* a strange beast for the people of this village,' she told Rasha.

'Thank you, Nani.'

'You know what I suggest? Explore the village on your own. Meet everyone. They won't bother you after that.'

'*Me?* On my own?'

Nani nodded.

'Will you come with me?'

'No.' Nani shook her head. 'I'm mad, and I don't like getting out of the house.'

'But I don't know the village at all!'

Almost as though he had come to solve this very problem, Jitu peeped into the room at that moment and asked anxiously, 'Is Rasha Apu sick? Is it cholera?'

'*Cholera? Me?*' asked Rasha in utter disbelief.

'Yes,' said Jitu, entering. 'Zobeda Fupu was on her way to meet you, but she didn't come because of your illness. "What's wrong," I asked her. Fupu said, "I don't know, but I think it's cholera. City people always have stomach problems when they come to the village. They get cholera."'

Rasha shook her head. 'No, I don't have cholera.'

'Then what do you have?'

'Nothing!'

'But—'

Rasha interrupted him. 'Can you do something for me, Jitu Mian?'

'Why not? Of course I can!'

Frowning, Rasha said, 'How can you say that without even knowing what I want you to do? What if I tell you to carry me on your shoulders to the market?'

Grinning, Jitu said, 'Stranger! You're stranger!'

Giving up, Rasha explained, 'I want to explore the village, visit everyone's homes. Will you come with me?'

Jitu's eyes brightened with joy. Slapping his thigh, he declared, 'Our house before anyone else's.'

'We'll see,' said Rasha.

Rasha realized when they went out together that there was no one better than Jitu for the job. Not only did he know every single inhabitant of the village, but he also knew each of the cows and sheep and goats and even the trees. He knew what each person was like, and he also knew the disposition of each of the animals.

As soon as they had left, he pointed to a cow in the distance, saying, 'See that black cow there? Never go near her.'

'Why not?' inquired Rasha.

'The cow is mad! She'll gore you if you go close to her.'

'How did she go mad?'

'I don't know. She broke free one night when there was no moon out and wandered off into the graveyard. I think she's been mad ever since.'

Rasha did not demand further explanation.

Stopping under a weeping tree, Jitu said, 'You mustn't walk under this tree at night.'

'Why not?'

'This is a fig tree. A ghost lives in it.'

'What does the ghost do?'

'It urinates on anyone passing below.'

Ghosts must have plenty of work of their own. Why they still had to lurk in a fig tree at night to urinate on people was beyond Rasha's comprehension. But she did not get into an argument with him, because she had realized by now that there was always a whiff of spirits and jinns and fairies about everything Jitu said.

The first house they visited had a large yard, where paddy stalks had been laid out to dry. Several birds were flying about, hoping to peck at the grains, while a young girl tried to shoo them away with a slender strip of bamboo. 'See who's a guess at your house, Shiuli,' Jitu told her.

'It's *guest*, not guess,' Rasha said quietly to Jitu, who showed no enthusiasm for perfecting his pronunciation. Instead, he said loudly, 'I've brought you a foreign guess, Safura Fupu.'

Rasha had no idea how *she* could be considered a foreigner. A crowd of people swarmed out from all over the house. Everyone knew who the foreign guest was, and were dying of curiosity about her. Before any of them could speak, Rasha said, 'I've never been here before, I don't know any of you. So I've come with Jitu Mian to meet all of you.'

An old woman stroked Rasha's head. 'I'm very glad, Ma. We've only heard of you, but never seen you. Now that we have, we're very happy.'

Rasha looked at her in surprise. It was clear from her expression that these were not mere words, that she had really meant what she'd said. The woman was indeed overwhelmed. She didn't know Rasha—she had never even seen her—and yet how happy she was to meet her. So strange! No one knew why, but suddenly a tear glistened in Rasha's eye. Hiding it and keeping her voice from breaking, she said, 'Since I'm new here, I don't know any of you. I'll get acquainted with all of you gradually.'

Another woman came up to her, saying affectionately, 'Will you actually stay, or will you just make us grow fond of you and then leave?'

'I'm staying,' reassured Rasha.

'What fun!' said one of the girls, clapping her hands.

The middle-aged woman said to someone, 'Fetch the stool. Let the girl sit.'

'Not today,' said Rasha. 'I want to visit everyone, I mustn't be late. I'll stay longer next time.'

'That doesn't mean you can go away without eating! You must have something.'

'No, no, nothing,' protested Rasha.

'You must!' The woman shook her head.

Rasha touched her hand. 'I've eaten already, believe me. Another day.'

'All right . . . but have a *daab* at least? You don't need an appetite for some coconut water.' Then she ordered a skinny little boy, '*Ei* Moti, go get a couple of daabs from the tree—quickly!'

Moti immediately hitched his lungi up around his waist, got an axe from somewhere and tucked it in at the back. Choosing one of the coconut trees in the yard, he shinned up the trunk. Rasha stared at him open-mouthed. Had she not seen it with her own eyes, she would never have believed that someone could climb a tree so easily. This boy named Moti seemed to be a lizard on a wall, not a human being.

Holding her breath, Rasha said, 'Oh Lord! What if he falls?'

'He won't,' said the little girl. 'Moti climbs trees like a monkey. He can leap from one to the next too.'

'Unbelievable,' said Rasha, her eyes bulging in astonishment.

Moti *did* actually climb the coconut tree like a monkey, taking the axe out of his waistband and skilfully severing a pair of daabs from their stalks before scuttling down again. He looked as though he found it easier to climb up and down trees than to walk.

Slicing the daab open at the head, Moti handed it to Rasha.

'How to drink this?' she asked.

'Hold it to your mouth,' said Moti.

'Really?'

'Really,' answered the dark-skinned boy, smiling with his pearl-white teeth.

Rasha tried to hold the daab to her mouth and drink the juice. But she spilled far more than she swallowed, soaking herself. The little children rolled on the ground with laughter. Rasha had never imagined it was possible to please anyone with so little.

A long time ago, when Rasha'd had chicken pox, she had been forced to drink daab juice. At that time she had thought of it as an unpleasant liquid with a foul smell. But the juice of this freshly cut daab was sweet and delicious—the flavour was lovely too. Rasha drank most of it quite willingly, and then said, 'Can't drink any more!'

The middle-aged woman said, 'Finish it, Jitu.'

Without demurring, Jitu held the daab to his mouth and gulped the rest down.

As she was about to leave, Rasha stopped abruptly. A baby with a swollen belly was sprawled in the veranda of a mud hut next door, without a stitch on him. Some *muri* was scattered on the floor in front of him, which he was picking out to eat, grain by grain and with rapt attention. A jackdaw nearby was trying to steal a share, hopping up quickly to gulp down a grain or two whenever the baby became careless.

Rasha gazed in wonder. Jitu asked, 'What's the matter, Rashapu?'

'Whose baby is that?'

A young woman standing nearby said, 'Mine.'

'Won't she fall ill if she eats food off the floor?'

With a troubled smile the baby's mother said, 'She won't. She's used to it.'

'But this is a very bad habit,' urged Rasha. 'There are *so* many germs on the floor. We have a microscope at school and our teacher showed us—there are germs everywhere, millions of them! Please give it to her in a bowl or on a plate.'

Sighing, the woman said, 'She gobbles it up from a bowl or a plate. It takes her much longer to pick out the grains if I scatter it on the floor . . .'

Rasha was taken aback. Hesitating, she insisted, 'But she'll fall ill if she eats off the floor.'

'What if she does? Everyone falls ill.'

Rasha stared at the woman in astonishment. What sort of reasoning was this? Not that she accepted the logic, though—instead, she forced the woman to remove the muri from the floor and give it to her daughter in a bowl. The funny thing, however, was that everyone there considered the whole thing an example of childishness on the part of a city-bred girl. They looked on smilingly, as though they were watching a play, but none of them seemed to take her seriously.

Rasha had visited the first house on her tour of the village with only Jitu for company but, when she left, she was joined by Moti and two other young children.

In the next house she discovered that they had already got to know that she was on her way and were waiting for her.

It was more or less a repetition of the same scene—everyone crowding around Rasha as though she was a princess from a foreign land who had wandered into the village by mistake. Here, too, she was made to sit on a stool and fed, *narkel naru* and *chinrebhaja* on a plate. Despite her refusal, she was forced to eat a naru and some chinre. By now she was aware that, here, eating had nothing to do with hunger or the desire for food. It was a social thing—people became upset if she refused.

Rasha felt the genuine affection of the village people but, at the same time, she could not understand their cruelty.

Just as she bit into a naru, one of the women said, 'So your father's left your mother and gone to London!'

Almost choking, Rasha replied, 'Not London, but Canada.'

'Where's that?'

'Near America.'

'So your father has married again?'

Rasha nodded.

'And your mother?' asked the woman.

Rasha stared at her in surprise and then found herself saying, 'Yes, so has she.'

'What does your stepfather do?'

'I don't know. I've never met him.'

The woman was about to ask some more questions when a girl of Rasha's age intervened. 'Can't you even let Rasha eat in peace, Ma? Give her time to eat instead of pestering her with a thousand questions!'

Taken aback, the woman stopped. Rasha looked gratefully at the frail girl, who followed her out as she was leaving. Taking Rasha's hand, she said, 'I hope you didn't mind.'

Although Rasha knew what she was talking about, she pretended not to, and asked, 'Didn't mind what?'

'My mother asking about your parents.'

'No,' Rasha shook her head. 'I didn't mind.'

The girl said gloomily, 'None of them have any sense . . . they don't know what to say. They're grown-up but they're silly. Like children.'

Rasha laughed at the other girl's anger. At least there was one person in the village with some common sense. 'What's your name?' she asked.

'Jainab.'

'Which class are you in?'

'I've made it to class seven. *Somehow*.'

'I'm in class eight,' Rasha told her. 'Which school do you go to?'

'Ahad Ali High School.'

'How far is it?'

'Quite far. At least three miles away. We can still get there now, but when it rains we can't go.'

'What's the school like?'

Jainab tried to smile. 'Like any village school—no studies to speak of. And the teachers won't give you marks in the exams unless you take private tuition from them.'

'I see.'

'I *go* to school, that's about it. I have no idea how long I'll be able to keep studying.'

'Why?'

'The school is so far away that my parents don't want me to go any more. "What does a girl need an education for," they say. Once I'm married I'll just have to cook the rest of my life anyway.'

About to protest, Rasha stopped herself. 'I see,' she said.

'Can I come with you?' asked Jainab, walking alongside.

'Yes, come!' said Rasha, pleased.

Rasha couldn't visit everyone that day but everywhere she went, Jainab protected her from two kinds of onslaughts. No one was allowed to ask her questions about her parents, and no one could force her to eat.

When Rasha returned home that evening, she discovered that there was at least one person in the village she could open her heart to.

The next day, Rasha visited the other houses in the village. Jainab was with her and Jitu joined them midway. Rasha came to know of several interesting things during her visits. For instance, that every village has a lunatic, who has to be tied up and who creates havoc if set free. There was such a madman in this village too—a *pagla* named Nur. They saw Nur Pagla from a distance, tethered to a palm tree with a rope. He was dressed in filthy clothes, his face was covered with an unkempt beard and he was muttering to himself. When he spotted Rasha and Jainab, he snarled threateningly at them.

Every village had a thief too, a *chor*. The one in this village was called Maqid Ali but everyone called him Makku Chora. Apparently he set out in the dead of night to steal things, oil smeared all over his body. Because he cared for his own village, he didn't steal here, taking his thieving ways to distant places instead. But whenever there was a theft in the nearby villages, the police arrested him. This was an annoyance.

As soon as Rasha asked Jitu what Makku Chora looked like, he took her and Jainab to his house. An emaciated man was sitting outside his door, smoking and making the hull of a boat with strips of bamboo. Apparently this was Makku Chora.

He peered suspiciously at them but Jitu explained, 'We have a foreign guess, Makku Chacha. I'm taking her around everyone's house!'

'I see,' said Makku Chora.

'Her father lives in London,' Rasha made no attempt to correct him.

'I see,' said Makku Chora.

'She's the granddaughter of the old teacher.'

'I see.'

'Her name is Rasha. She lives in a city, you see, so her name is Itis Mitis.'

Makku Chora said, 'I see.'

Who knows what Jitu might have said now to continue the conversation, but a very pretty woman now emerged from the house to interrupt it anyway. Rasha had never seen anyone so beautiful.

Jitu said, 'I've brought a foreign guess, Chachi.'

The pretty woman said, 'You've brought your guest to a poor man's house. I can't even offer her a seat.'

'No,' Rasha said, 'we won't be sitting. We'll go now. We have to visit a lot of people.'

As they walked off, Rasha turned around to look behind her. The pretty woman stood there, her hand on the door. Holding her breath, Rasha whispered to Jainab, 'How pretty she is!'

'Yes,' said Jainab. 'Very pretty.'

'How did a thief manage to marry such a beautiful woman?'

'No idea.'

'Doesn't she tell her husband not to steal?'

'I don't know. Who listens to their wife anyway?'

Just like a lunatic and a thief, every village also had some people who were up to no good. They ran into one such person on the road. He was dressed in tight trousers, a gaudy red T-Shirt and dark glasses. Standing by the road, he was combing his hair. He turned to look at Rasha, Jainab and Jitu as they passed.

As Jitu and Jainab were about to cross him, he stopped them and asked, 'Is that you, Jitu? Who's this with you?'

'Rashapu. The teacher's granddaughter.'

'I see.'

'She's here from Dhaka.'

'*From Dhaka to this village?* This isn't a place for human beings! No electricity, no television.'

Rasha didn't say a word.

The man said, 'I'm won't be staying here.'

'Where will you go?' Jitu inquired.

'Abroad. Got my passport.'

'When are you going?'

'Haven't fixed the date yet. I'll go to Dubai. It's huge. Money floats in the air there—just catch it and put in your pocket!' He mimed the act.

'We'll go now,' said Jainab.

She tugged at Rasha's hand and the three of them set off. Behind them, the man said, 'Give my salaam to your father. I'll visit your house one of these days with the new officer in charge.'

'Who was that?' Rasha asked softly.

'Faltu Majid. There are two Majids in the village—this one is the useless one, *faltu*. The real Majid has a shop in the market. This one does no work, only talks big.'

Rasha smiled derisively, saying, 'Did you see his clothes? A complete joker!'

'Yes, he's combing his hair all the time!'

Jainab stopped abruptly on the dusty village road. Rasha saw a large tree next to a pond and a man who sat leaning against the tree, reading a book with close attention. He was probably short-sighted, for he was holding the volume very close to his eyes. Their chatter didn't break his concentration.

Going up to him, Jainab and Jitu said, 'Salamalaikum, Chachaji.'

Now the man raised his eyes. His hair was grey and he was wearing glasses. 'Walaikum salaam, Jainab Beti. Walaikum salaam, Jitu Mian,' he answered. 'Who is this girl with you?'

'The teacher's granddaughter,' said Jainab.

'Rashapu,' added Jitu.

Sitting up straight, the man dog-eared the page he was reading and said, 'You're Aziz Master's granddaughter? Come closer, let me look at you properly.'

Rasha went up to him. Taking her hand, he made her sit down and scanned her face. Then a soft smile suffused his own. 'You resemble Aziz Bhaisaab,' he said.

Rasha hesitated, unsure of how to respond. 'Did you know my grandfather?' she asked.

The man smiled. 'That's putting it mildly. Your nana was very close to me. Do you know when the strongest friendship is formed between two people? When they fight side by side. Your nana and I fought in the war together—the *muktijuddho*. He was our commander.'

Gazing at the water in the pond, the man took off his glasses and wiped his eyes with the corner of his shirt. 'We felt as though our world had ended when they took your nana away after he was caught.'

Rasha looked at him in surprise. She suddenly realized that she had no idea what sort of man her grandfather had been, or how he had died.

Sighing, the man said, his mind clearly elsewhere, 'I had warned Aziz Bhai. I had told him not to return. But your mother had just been born and he was desperate to see her! He was caught as soon as he went home. What a blow it was for bhaabi. Poor thing—she lost her sanity overnight.'

Rasha knew none of this. She was dying to know more but she didn't ask any questions, sitting in front of the man in silence. He said, 'Sometimes I feel very guilty when I think of the fact that I'm living in the same country that your grandfather sacrificed his life for.'

'Why should you feel guilty? asked Rasha.

'I shouldn't have to—but I do. What to do?' His voice changed. 'Go on, Ma, go on wherever it was you were going. I'm getting old, you see. It makes me want to talk to people of your age. And you are . . .?'

'Rasha.'

'Yes, *Rasha*. You're Aziz Bhai's granddaughter. Which makes you my granddaughter too! I'm your Salam Nana.'

'Salam Nana?'

'Yes. Aziz Nana's friend, Salam Nana.' Putting his hand on Rasha's head, the man said, 'I'm an old man, so you can call me Nana. But the word doesn't suit Aziz Bhai. He was twenty-three or twenty-four when he became a martyr—in the prime of life. As handsome as a prince. Thick black hair and, since he couldn't shave during the war, he had a beard like Che

Guevara's. He didn't grow old like I did. You mustn't call him Nana.'

'What should I call him then?'

'Bhai. Aziz Bhai.' Leaning back against the tree, he looked at Rasha smilingly through his thick glasses.

As she was leaving, Rasha noticed a pair of crutches propped up against the tree. Wooden crutches, smoothened with constant use. Salam Nana had lost his legs.

Jainab explained later, 'Salam Chacha was a freedom fighter from our village. He was shot in the legs during the war and they had to amputate them. So he has to use crutches.'

'I see,' said Rasha.

'We had two freedom fighters in our village. The first *muktijodhha* is your nana—'

'My bhai,'

Jainab smiled. 'Yes, your bhai, a martyr. And the other is our Salam Chacha.'

'Are there any *razakars* in this village?'

'No, there's no one in this village who fought for the Pakistan Army. There's someone in the next village though.'

'What's his name?'

'Ahad Ali.'

It was a name Rasha had heard before, though she couldn't remember where.

The Ramshackle School

'There's our school,' said Jainab.

A huge, weeping tree stood at the end of the village road they were walking on, shading some tin buildings. There was an open field in front of it, where several children were running about, playing.

Rasha had come to see the school with the children of the village. This was the school she would have to attend if she wanted to study. It was quite far—at least three miles away—and it had taken her an hour to walk here.

A little further on, she noticed a signboard with the name of the school written on it in large letters—*Ahad Ali High School.*

'Who's Ahad Ali?' Rasha asked Jainab.

'A VIP from the next village. Very rich.'

'You'd said there's a razakar in the next village named Ahad Ali!'

'Same man.'

'*Same man?*' Rasha was astonished. 'A school named after a razakar?'

Jainab nodded glumly. 'It seems everyone's forgotten he was a razakar. He's built a school, a madrasah too. Filthy rich.'

'How did he do all this?'

'I'm not sure. During the war he grabbed the land owned by Hindus. That's how he became rich.'

Rasha stared at the signboard in bewilderment. Her grandfather had been martyred in the war for freedom, and now she was expected to go to a school named after a razakar? For shame!

Jainab went off to deposit her books in the classroom. Rasha peeped in. It was hard to believe a classroom could be so miserable. Benches of cheap wood had been knocked together somehow, looking like they would collapse any moment. The bricks in the wall were visible and the blackboard was faded. The floor had been paved in the dim distant past but it was pockmarked with holes now, besides being littered with scraps of paper and leaves, and layered with dust. The students began arriving. Most of them didn't even have shoes. There was no uniform—everyone dressed as they pleased, so that it didn't feel like a school at all. The emaciated appearance of the boys and girls made it obvious that they were from poor families.

Jainab took Rasha to the headmaster's room. An old man was bent over a notebook on a desk in the corner of the small room. According to Jainab, this was the headmaster.

'May I come in, sir?' Rasha asked from the door.

'Who's that?' said the headmaster without raising his eyes.

Unsure of what to say, Rasha hesitated. Then she said, 'I'm here to talk to you about something, sir.'

Now the headmaster looked up. He seemed surprised to see Rasha.

'Come in,' he said. 'Talk about what?'

'I want to find out how to take admission in your school, sir,' Rasha said.

The headmaster stared at Rasha in astonishment. He had never in his entire life had a student come to him on their own to ask to be enrolled in school. There was always an adult accompanying them.

'Where are your parents?' the headmaster asked.

'Abroad.'

'Abroad, where?'

Rasha sighed mentally. She would now have to recount the entire history—in which case she might as well be straightforward instead of beating about the bush. So she said candidly, 'My father is in Canada. My mother, in Australia. I've been left behind with my grandmother in the village here. Since this is where I'll have to live, I've come here to be admitted to your school.'

Still staring at Rasha, the headmaster said, 'Don't you have any other guardian besides your grandmother?'

'No.'

'Which class do you want to be enrolled in?'

'Class eight.'

There was no rush of students at the school, but the headmaster put up an act. 'There's a shortage of seats,' he said. 'It's difficult to get admitted in the middle of the year.'

'I know, sir,' said Rasha, 'but I have no choice.'

'Let me see what I can do. But there are expenses—admission fees to be paid, monthly fees too. Who will pay all this?'

'I will, sir. I'll bring it if you tell me how much it is.'

A fleeting expression of greed appeared in the headmaster's eyes. Softly, he said, 'Fees for the previous months. Admission fees. Special fees. Contingency fees. About three or four thousand in all . . .'

Exhaling in apprehension, Rasha said, 'All right, sir.'

Someone else entered the headmaster's room now—a young, well-built man with a light beard.

'I'm glad to see you, Razzak,' said the headmaster. 'This girl wants to get admitted to class eight.'

The man named Razzak turned around and then asked, 'Who's she here with?'

'She's come on her own. Family problems.'

Razzak took a good look at Rasha, who realized at once that he had taken a dislike to her.

'What have you told her?' Razzak asked the headmaster.

'I've told her to bring the money for the fees and get herself admitted.'

Razzak shook his head. 'No, sir. We can't do it that way.'

'We have seats, what's the problem?' the headmaster asked feebly.

'The problem is elsewhere.'

'Where?'

'This girl is here without her parents. Do you know anything about her? What if she's run away from home? You might find yourself implicated and dragged into a police case if you admit her. Do you know how dangerous today's boys and girls are?'

Rasha listened in astonishment, unable to speak.

'It's obvious,' continued Razzak. 'All these city boys and girls are on drugs. You'll take her in blindly and, the next thing you know, half the children in this village school have become drug addicts! Terrible times, sir.'

'Of course I'm not a drug addict,' Rasha tried to protest.

Looking at her, Razzak said, 'The headmaster and I are talking—who asked you to butt in?'

'Since it's me you're discussing . . .'

Razzak glared at Rasha before turning back to the headmaster.

'You see how impertinent she is? Talking back! You want to admit a girl like her? She'll ruin your school.'

The headmaster said, 'Anyway, since we have seats, let's admit her. Now, tell me under what rule you are willing to admit her.'

'It won't be right to admit her without a transfer certificate, exam results, a testimonial from the head of her previous school and a photo ID from the last school. Otherwise, you'll get into trouble afterwards, sir.'

'This girl's parents live abroad. She has no guardian and lives with her old grandmother. How will she get hold of all these documents?'

'That's not our concern, sir. It's hers. Let her get the documents before she's admitted. No documents, no admission!'

The headmaster tried to smile tentatively at Rasha. 'Did you hear? You cannot be admitted till you get the transfer certificate, the exam results, a testimonial and a photo ID from the previous school.'

Rasha was about to put on a forlorn expression and make a request, but she had no desire to do it in Razzak's presence.

'Very well, sir,' she said in a subdued voice.

Jainab had been standing outside, looking worried. 'Done?' she asked.

'No.' Rasha shook her head.

'Why not?'

'The headmaster was willing. But a teacher named Razzak came in and spoilt everything! He mentioned all sorts of documents.'

'Do you have them?'

'*How* will I have them?'

'What will you do then?'

Rasha sighed. 'Let me see. I have to talk to my teacher at my last school.'

'How will you do that?'

'I'll probably have to write her a letter.'

'Don't you have her phone number?'

'I do.' Jahanara Madam *had* given Rasha her phone number, asking her to call if necessary. She had memorized it. She had often thought of calling but, for some reason or the other, hadn't got around to it.

'Call her at once in that case,' urged Jainab.

'Call from where?'

'There's a phone-and-fax shop in the market. Let me take you there.'

'Don't you have classes any minute now?'

'Doesn't matter—I can miss them for once!'

As Jainab set off with Rasha, Jitu came out of his classroom to join them. He didn't enjoy school at all, running away whenever he could.

Dialling the number, Rasha heard the phone ring, followed by a click. Then Jahanara Madam's voice said, 'Hello.'

'It's Rasha, madam.'

Jahanara Madam was silent for a few moments before asking apprehensively, 'Where are you, Rasha?'

'I'm at my nani's house.'

'Where is your nani's house?'

'You won't know this place, madam. It's a village deep in the countryside.'

'Why are you there? How long will you stay?'

'My mother has left me here to get married and move to Australia.'

There was a long silence on the other side. Then Jahanara Madam said, 'You didn't tell me anything, Rasha.'

'What use would it have been, madam?' said Rasha, blinking back tears. 'How can anyone help someone who's abandoned by her own mother this way?'

'How are you now?' said Jahanara Madam. 'What are you up to?'

'I'm all right. I need some documents to get admitted to a school here. That's why I've called you.'

'What documents?'

'A transfer certificate, a testimonial, a mark sheet and a photo ID. I have a photo ID. I need the other three.'

'All right. Is there a fax nearby?'

'I'm calling from a shop with a fax.'

'Good. Give me the number. I'm faxing you everything in half an hour. I'll courier one set of originals to your school and another to your grandmother's house.'

'All right, madam.'

'Do give me the fax number. And the addresses.'

'Yes, madam. Thank you, madam.'

'Rasha, listen.'

'Yes, madam?'

'You must keep in touch with me. All right?'

'I will, madam. Pray for me, madam.'

There was no reply.

Half an hour later, the headmaster of Ahad Ali High School was amazed to see the girl seeking admission, back in his room, holding a set of documents.

'What is it?' he asked.

'The documents you'd asked for, sir. My school has faxed them over. The originals have been couriered as well, they'll be here in a day or day two.'

Examining the documents, the headmaster discovered that the girl was a very talented student. She had won a national-level prize at the Mathematics Olympiad, and was an excellent debater and elocutionist. She was taking a transfer from the school because of family problems—and a request was being made to help her. The headmistress of her previous school had written a letter, asking to be contacted in case more information was required. She had said that Rasha was a gem of a girl. She was, after all, the headmistress of a famous school—even the headmaster had heard of her.

The headmaster rose to his feet with the documents, taking Rasha to the next room. A clerk was sitting amidst a pile of files, chewing some paan. He shot up on seeing the headmaster.

Handing him the faxes, the headmaster said, 'Haripada, make the arrangements to admit this girl to class eight.'

'Admission fees?'

'Later. She'll pay it in a day or two. Make sure she doesn't have to pay a single extra paisa!'

Razzak appeared suddenly. Taking the documents from the clerk, he scanned them quickly. 'These are faxes, sir. These are useless! She can't be admitted without the originals. Besides, there is the matter of fees too.'

This time the headmaster didn't give in. Looking stern, he said, 'I've been a headmaster for twenty years, Razzak Sahib. I know when originals are needed and when faxes will do. And if this girl cannot pay her fees, I will! *Understood?*'

Razzak's face fell at this humiliation.

Rasha said hesitantly, 'I'll pay the admission fees. I'll bring the money tomorrow.'

'I know you will, Ma,' said the headmaster. 'Start classes tomorrow. This village school is in a bad way. The building is worn out and so are the teachers. The standards are not every high. You'll find it difficult to study here. But it all depends on you. Vidyasagar used to study by the light of a lamp post. Do you follow me?'

'*Ji*, sir. I do.'

Rasha hadn't left. The headmaster asked, 'Is there something else you want to say?'

'Ji, sir.'

'Tell me.'

'I have walked a long way here with several others. And I'll walk back with them later—so I'll have to wait in any case. May I start classes today?'

'Why not? Of course you may! Come with me.'

Rasha followed the headmaster. Classes had begun. A teacher was caning a student in one of the classrooms, the swish of the cane synchronized with the student's shrieks. It seemed to be an everyday occurrence, because the headmaster didn't even seem to hear it.

The headmaster stopped in front of a classroom in the corner. The boys and girls stood up when they saw him. A dark, bald teacher was writing on the blackboard. He stopped and turned towards the headmaster. Entering with Rasha, he told the children to sit down. Then he said to the teacher, 'This girl is joining class eight, Mazhar Sahib. Haripada is getting the papers in order but let her start at once.'

'Very well, sir.'

The headmaster then addressed the students. 'This girl is new to your class and she's a brilliant student. All of you *must* help her. All right?'

The students nodded like robots. After the headmaster had left, the dark, bald man looked at Rasha for a while through slitted eyes. Then he said, 'Name?'

'Everyone calls me Rasha.'

'Rasha?'

'Ji, sir.'

'Rasha isn't the name of a girl, it's the name of a country! That's how Russia is pronounced.'

A few of the children laughed, then stopped abruptly. Rasha stood in silence.

'You should have been named Raisa instead of Rasha,' the teacher said. 'The name Raisa means something—Rasha has no meaning.'

Rasha didn't respond this time either. The less she said, the better.

'Sit down,' the teacher said.

A girl sitting on the front bench made room for Rasha. The teacher approached the blackboard again with his chalk. He was doing a sum on the board. He completed it without a word and the students copied it down.

When he had finished, the teacher turned to face the class. 'Have all of you taken it down?'

'Yes, sir.'

He proceeded to wipe the board clean and start on a new sum. Rasha observed that he wasn't working it out—he was merely copying it from a book in his hand! How strange!

The entire period passed this way. The teacher wrote out one sum after another on the blackboard, and the children noted everything down. So this was how mathematics was taught here.

Eventually the bell rang, and the teacher left with his notebooks and register. The boys and girls began to talk in a low voice. The girls on the same bench as Rasha were looking at her covertly but hadn't yet summoned the courage to talk to her. Rasha started a conversation herself, with the pretty girl next to her.

'What's your name?' Rasha asked her.

'Sanjida.'

'My best friend in my last school was named Sanjida!'

The girl gazed at her without replying.

Rasha asked, 'Do you also think that no one can be called Rasha?'

Sanjida nodded. 'They can. How could you be named Rasha otherwise?'

'Can I tell you something?'

Sanjida nodded again. 'Yes, tell me.'

'Promise not to tell anyone?'

'I won't tell anyone.'

'You swear on the Lord?'

'I swear on the Lord,' Sanjida said, a little surprised.

Several other students came up to Rasha now—everyone wanted to hear her secret.

Lowering her voice, Rasha said, 'Actually my name *was* Raisa. I couldn't stand it—so I changed it to Rasha.'

The girls stared at one another. It had never occurred to them that you could change your name if you didn't like it.

One of the girls asked, 'If you don't like this name either, will you change it again?'

Rasha smiled. 'No more changes,' she said.

'But Raisa is quite a nice name—why did you change it?' asked the girl.

'There's a reason.'

'What reason?'

'There was a very naughty boy in our class who had made up a rhyme about me.'

'What rhyme?'

'First you must promise not to tease me . . .'

'Promise.'

'Swear on the Lord?'

'Swear on the Lord.'

'The rhyme went—*Raisa . . . Eats her fish with rice-a . . .*'

The girls laughed loudly, which made some of the boys look their way to find out what was so funny.

'Aren't there any naughty boys in your class?' asked Rasha.

The girls exchanged glances. 'We don't know.'

'You don't know! Why not?'

'We don't talk to the boys. The boys stick to themselves, the girls too.'

'You've *never* spoken to them?' Rasha asked in astonishment.

'No.'

'Why not?'

The girls didn't reply. No one seemed to know *why* the boys and the girls didn't talk to one another. It had always been this way.

Suddenly there was an uproar in the boys' section. Everyone was trying to push one of them forward. He seemed reluctant but no one could be bothered.

'What's going on?' Rasha asked the girls.

'This boy sings beautifully. They're probably asking him to sing.'

'Sing? Now? Don't we have class?'

'No. The English teacher hasn't come in a long time.'

'Why not?'

'We don't know. Apparently he's gone off to London.'

'Gone off to London?' Rasha asked in surprise. 'Shouldn't someone else be taking the class then?'

'As if there's anyone else! No teachers.'

The boy who could sing was about to return to his seat when Rasha spoke up. 'Sing for us, please!'

The entire class fell silent. No girl had ever spoken to a boy in this classroom. No one spoke for a while. Then someone said, 'Yes, Gazi. Sing for us.'

The rest joined in., 'Yes, sing for us!'

Just as a commotion was about to start, one of the boys said, 'Quiet! Don't shout or else Razzak Sir will turn up with his cane.'

When the noise died down, Gazi stepped forward shyly. He seemed nervous. Standing in front, he shut his eyes and began to sing. Everyone fell silent again. Such a beautiful voice, such control over rhythm. Rasha was stunned. With his eyes closed, he sang—

> It's too late to show your devotion now
> Where was it when there was still time . . .

It seemed that this young boy had really wanted to dedicate himself to something but hadn't done it in time, and was heartbroken now.

Everyone clapped in appreciation when the song ended.

'How beautifully you sing!' Rasha gushed.

None of the boys in the class knew how to respond to a girl. The boy who had sung remained silent.

'Do you learn music?' Rasha asked.

'No.' The boy shook his head.

'Then how did you learn to sing so well?'

'By myself.'

'By yourself! *How?*'

'They play songs at Subal's tea shop, that's how I learnt.'

'That's amazing! You sing so well without any lessons. Imagine how much more beautifully you could sing if you had an ustad to train you.'

'Ustad! *Tchah!*' said someone from the back.

'Why not?' asked Rasha.

'If Gazi's father comes to know that he's singing, he'll break all his bones!'

'*Why?*'

'His father is a fundamentalist.'

'Can't a fundamentalist listen to music?'

'*His* father doesn't,' said the boy in the back row.

The other boys asked Gazi for one more song. He had overcome his shyness by now. Now he sang one of Hason Raja's folk songs. As he was returning to his seat afterwards, Rasha said, 'You sing so marvellously! If I'd had some money, I'd encase your throat in gold.'

Rasha wasn't joking but everyone giggled in joy—though no one knew what they were happy about.

When the bell rang, Razzak Sir came into the classroom with a long cane. Rasha sighed. Who knew which boy or girl he was going to use the cane on? He might cane her too, she wondered.

Razzak Sir walked around the classroom brandishing his weapon. Then he asked whether everyone had prepared their science lessons. The boys and girls sat in silence. The teacher proceeded to quiz them, starting from one corner of the room. Whoever got the answer right was let off, but anyone who got it wrong was caned unmercifully. Razzak

Sir's lower lip protruded during the beating, and a slurping sound emerged from his mouth. How ghastly!

Soon Rasha discovered something. The teacher let the student off if the answer was right, and caned him or her if it was wrong—but only *he* decided which answer was right and which, wrong. A boy whose answer was patently incorrect remained unscathed, while another one was caned viciously despite giving the correct answer. Although Rasha knew it was risky talking in class, she couldn't help asking Sanjida, 'Sir's caning some of the students even when they give the right answer. And even though some are getting their answers wrong . . .'

'There's no right or wrong,' Sanjida answered softly. 'Sir canes everyone who doesn't take private tuition from him.'

'He canes all those who don't take private tuition?'

'Yes.'

'Do you take private tuition?'

'I do.'

'So you won't be caned?'

'No. But Shiuli will.'

'Shiuli doesn't take private tuition?'

'No.'

'What about me?' Rasha asked.

'Since it's your first day, sir will probably let you off.'

Sanjida proved to be right. The teacher spared her but Shiuli was caned. He told Rasha that he was letting her off because it was her first day, but that he wouldn't do so the next time.

Gazi, the boy who had sung, was thrashed unmercifully. Rasha realized that the teacher's methods were simple. He would take care of those who took private tuition . He would tell them the questions in advance, give them good marks and not cane them in class. But those who did not go to him for tuition would be beaten till they reformed.

Rasha cast a long, cold look at the monster in the classroom.

The First Punishment

Rasha finally unlocked her suitcase after several days. She had brought all her essential things in it. She remembered putting in a few textbooks at the last minute; now she took them out. She didn't have all the books needed for school—some would have to be bought locally. She even found two notebooks after scouring the suitcase. There was enough for school the next day.

Spreading them out on the bed, Rasha was leafing through the pages when Nani came to sit beside her.

'You'll need a desk and a chair to study, won't you?' she said.

'There's no hurry, Nani. Vidyasagar used to study under the street lights—at least I have my own lamp.'

'It's all been very difficult for you, hasn't it?'

'I won't lie to you, Nani—yes, it has. I've never walked such a long distance as I did today. My feet are aching.'

'Let me see them, I'll give you a massage.'

Rasha giggled. 'What rubbish, Nani! Why will you massage my feet? I'd rather you patted me on the back and said, "Well done, my girl!"'

And so Nani patted her on the back, saying, 'Well done, my girl!' Then she added, 'You're my worthy granddaughter. You've joined school without anyone's help.'

'Now pat me on my back again and kiss my forehead.'

Nani patted her on the back and gave her lots of kisses.

Sighing, Rasha said, 'You must never ask me to tell you the name of my school. All right, Nani?'

'Why not?'

'The school has been named after a razakar. I will never utter a razakar's name!'

Nani kept looking at Rasha without a word.

Rasha said, 'Considering that Nana was such a renowned freedom fighter, I cannot possibly go to a school named after a razakar. The name will *have* to be changed!'

'How will you change it?'

'I don't know.' Turning to Nani, Rasha said, 'Don't you remember the amulet you gave me, which can grant wishes?'

'Yes, I do.'

'This is what I'll wish for.'

'All right.'

After a while Rasha said, 'Nani.'

'What is it?'

'Ammu has never told me *anything* about Nana. I know nothing about him! Will you tell me some day?'

Nani looked at Rasha, and her eyes lost focus. Her hands began to tremble. She whispered, 'Don't ask me to, shona. My head feels strange when I think of those days. I can't control myself.'

Rasha realized, to her surprise, that everything had once turned upside down for Nani. Nani sat there helplessly, trembling violently. A fearful Rasha put her arms around her grandmother. 'Sorry, Nani, sorry! I didn't know. I'll never ask again. I swear by the Lord, Nani. *Never.*'

Handing a list to the shopkeeper, Rasha asked, 'Do you have these books?'

Examining the list, the man said, 'We do.'

'May I have them, please?'

He pulled those out and some others from the shelves, and pushed them towards Rasha.

Placing the prescribed textbooks on one side, Rasha pointed to the rest, asking, 'What are these?'

'We don't sell textbooks unless you buy the guide books too.'

'What do you mean? I'll take only the books I want.'

The man said, 'How much money can we make by selling textbooks alone? Our profits come from the guide books. If you want to buy your books, you must take the guide books too. I'll give you a fifty per cent discount!'

'I'll never buy guidebooks,' declared Rasha.

'Then you'll never be able to buy textbooks! No one in this country sells textbooks alone.'

'Says who?'

'It's the truth,' Jainab whispered to Rasha, clutching her elbow.

'The truth?'

'Yes. All of us had to buy guidebooks.'

Rasha looked at the shopkeeper through narrowed eyes. Then she said, 'All right, give me the whole lot.'

He brought the books down from the shelf again.

'How much?' asked Rasha.

The shopkeeper added up the figures on a piece of paper and told Rasha. Paying, she said, 'Do you have a pair of scissors?'

'Scissors?'

'Yes.'

'Why?'

'I need them.'

The shopkeeper found a large pair beneath the counter and handed them to her. Rasha began to cut up the pages of the guide books.

'What do you think you're doing?' the man protested.

'I'm cutting up the pages!'

'But why?'

'I want them in small pieces. Then I'll give them to the *chanachur* seller on the street! He'll make paper cones with them.'

'You're wasting the books you paid for?'

'I'm not wasting them at all. I'm putting them to good use. This is how one *should* use guide books.'

The shopkeeper said impatiently, 'If you want to waste them give them back to me instead!'

'I told you—I'm *not* wasting them, I'm putting them to use. Selling these guide books to students amounts to wasting them.'

With great care, Rasha continued cutting up the pages into small pieces. The shopkeeper stared in wonder as she handed the pieces to the chanachur seller outside.

'What's all this?' he asked.

'You can use these to make cones to serve your chanachur in,' Rasha told him.

He seemed unsure. These pieces of paper were larger than the ones he used. He stood holding them, not sure of what to do.

Rasha led Jainab away quickly. Even if the chanachur seller threw the pieces of paper away, they would have proved useful, thought Rasha.

Again the bald mathematics teacher copied sums from a book in his hand on to the blackboard. Again the English teacher didn't show up. Gazi sang two songs and a boy named Matin did a comic act. It was childish but Rasha pretended to laugh. Razzak Sir came for the science class, once again brandishing his cane. Putting it down on the desk, he walked up and down the classroom several times before turning to the students and saying, 'I'm going to say a few things today. Listen carefully.'

The class sat up.

Razzak Sir said, 'When *we* were in school, we were particularly respectful to our teachers. We would greet them every time we ran into them. If we came across a teacher with a shopping bag, we would carry it home for them. But now—?'

Glaring at the students, the teacher continued, 'Far from greeting me, the other day a student pretended to not even see me and slipped into a lane. Did he think I didn't see him? I did—and I'll take his skin off with a whip one day.'

Looking grim, he went on. 'The future of this country is bleak. Good people aren't born here any more—only criminals and scoundrels. This nation does not respect its teachers. Their salaries are so low that their families cannot survive. Still, I chose to be a teacher. Do you understand me? If I can nurture even one good person among all the criminals and scoundrels, I'll consider that my life as a teacher has been successful. Do you understand?'

The students nodded mechanically. The teacher said, 'It takes a lot of time to teach a subject properly. Does anyone give us the time we need? They don't. That's why we cannot complete the course in class. Other teachers give up, but I don't! I teach at home too. Those who take private tuition from me do well in exams. I research the past three or four years' board examinations to suggest questions. And they work! I could have sold these suggestions for lakhs of taka if I'd wanted to. But I don't. I pass them on to my students.'

Snorting, he continued, 'So those of you who want to do well in your examinations, who want to study hard and be successful, *must* come to my house after classes for tuition. Will you remember that?'

Everyone nodded mechanically again. The teacher said, 'And I will assume that those who *don't* come, have no interest in their studies. There will be no mercy for them. Understand?' The students nodded to indicate that they had understood. Then Razzak Sir began to teach, asking the students to read out from the textbook by turn. To those who went to him for tuition, he said, 'Very good'. Those who didn't, were caned for not reading well.

Rasha was not used to seeing a teacher thrash a student. Her skin prickled at the sight. She shut her eyes, for she couldn't bear it any more. It was impossible!

The following week could be considered a very important one in Rasha's life. The first reason was a package from Jahanara Madam. She had told Rasha on the phone that she would send two sets of original documents—one to the school and one to Rasha's grandmother's house. So Rasha had been expecting a thin, ordinary envelope, but what arrived was a large parcel! Since it had been sent by registered post, Rasha not only had to sign for it but also give a tip to the peon.

Besides the documents she needed for admission, the packet contained two books and a letter. The letter was from Jahanara Madam, and it brought tears to Rasha's eyes. Madam had written—

Dear Rasha,

I haven't written many letters in my life but I thought I'd write you one. I could have told you all this on the telephone too, but I felt it would be better to write to you instead. There are many things that cannot be said aloud, they can only be written in a letter. And then there are many other things that cannot be written in a letter but only said.

I have been teaching for a long time. I have had many students, some of whom have accomplished great things. You were one among all these students; I didn't consider you any different from the rest. I didn't believe you the first day you told me that your mother would abandon you and leave, but you had planted a seed of doubt in my mind. Children often have a sixth sense about such things. When you suddenly stopped coming to school and I had no news even after making enquiries, I was overcome with a sharp sense of guilt. I felt like you had come to me for help, but that I hadn't helped you.

When you called suddenly, I was petrified with fear. I had no idea what you would tell me. You could have told me that your mother had abandoned you in a remote village at your grandmother's home—that your studies were done with, that your life was over. It wouldn't have been untrue. But that was not what you told me. What you told me was that you were alone—yes, completely alone in this dreadful time. But that you were preparing to continue your studies at an unknown school in a remote village. Whom should I salute if not you?

The school I teach in is one of the most famous ones in Bangladesh. The students do well in their exams every year; their photographs appear in the papers. But I know that we don't give them an education—we only teach them how to get good marks. So is it really much of a loss to be studying in an unknown school in a remote village instead of a reputed one? I don't think so. My students are at school all day, and then spend their evenings taking private lessons. Can there be a more joyless life? At least you don't have to live this way. I imagine you can see the trees, you can see the sky, you can see the rice fields and the river. I'm sure you will see the full moon, you will see the moonbeams. It has been a long time since we in the city have seen them.

Your education depends on you. I have been a teacher for twenty years but I have not taught anyone anything. Whatever my students have learnt, they have learnt on their own. I have only encouraged them to learn. So I'm writing this letter to encourage you. I'm sending you three books. The first is a mathematics textbook. It has everything you will need till the time you go to university. You must read the chapters, go over the examples and solve the problems at the end of every chapter. The day you are done with this book, you can pat yourself on the back and say, 'Rasha! You have indeed learnt all the mathematics one needs, to succeed in life!'

The second book is a physics textbook. If you read the introduction, you'll find that it's been written for college students. But I've observed that anyone can read and understand it. If you can finish it, I'll personally kiss you on your cheeks. It'll help you enormously—you'll never have trouble with school-level science again.

The third book is an anthology of English short stories. It has stories by the best writers in the world. It's not meant for a girl of thirteen or fourteen at all—but then I do not think of you as a thirteen- or fourteen-year-old girl. You *have grown up very quickly. Who knows, maybe you're more grown-up than I am.. I'm sending you this book because you must keep practising your English.*

I haven't been to a village in a long time—perhaps the villages are no longer as they used to be. Dirty politics and irrational policies and religious restrictions must have made inroads by now. You must be very careful. If you need help—of any kind—you must ask me. Memorize my phone number, all right?

Yours,
Jahanara Madam

Rasha read the letter thrice in succession and then, folding it, wept a little. These were not tears of frustration and despair—these were different. Then she turned to the books. They weren't cheap, pirated photocopies, but beautiful, shiny foreign editions. The fresh smell of new books was on every page. Such lovely silky paper, dazzling printing, bright pictures—one would want to clasp the books to their breast. She leafed through them for a long time. She had no desk or shelf for her books, so she put them under her pillow, running her fingertips over them whenever she had a few moments.

The other reason for which the week proved very significant for Rasha was completely different—she was caned for the first time in her life. She had never imagined that someone would hit her, but that was just what happened.

Razzak Sir had come into the classroom with his cane, as he did every day. Putting it on the desk, he blabbered for some time before pretending to teach. Then, under the pretext of testing the students, he began to thrash them. He was in an especially bad mood today for some reason, which made him cane them even more ferociously. Halfway through the class, one of the boys—unable to take the beating any more, tried to shield himself with his arms. The outcome was catastrophic. The teacher grew even more furious, dragging the boy by a fistful of his hair and flinging him on to a bench to beat him so savagely that he seemed ready to kill him.

Rasha couldn't take it any more. Without even being aware of what she was doing, she leapt up and shouted at the top of her voice, 'Sir!'

A bomb seemed to go off. The teacher let go of the boy's hair and turned around. His eyes were fiery, his nostrils flaring; his lower jaw had dropped, so that his teeth were showing.

'Who was that?' he said violently.

'Me, sir,' said Rasha.

'What is it?'

'You cannot beat him up this way.'

The teacher looked as though he couldn't believe his ears. 'What did you say?' he barked.

'I said you cannot beat him up this way in the classroom.'

The teacher's eyes blazed redder. He seemed ready to breath fire. Clutching his cane, he came up to Rasha, saying, '*You're* teaching *me* what to do? How dare you!'

'It's not a question of daring, sir, it's—'

The teacher emitted a roar, not allowing Rasha to finish. 'You dare talk back to me?'

'No, sir. It's just that—' Rasha stopped abruptly. Razzak Sir was standing in front of her now, so close that she could smell his feral stench.

Glaring at Rasha, he said, 'You brazen girl! I'll teach you a lesson for life today . . .'

Rasha didn't speak. She had suddenly realized that something horrific was going to take place.

'Hold out your hand . . .' said the teacher.

Rasha held out her hand, palm upturned. The teacher raised his cane, Rasha saw it swooping down to her hand—and then there was a crack. She felt as though her palm had been set on fire. A sharp, shooting pain spread through her whole body. She felt an irresistible urge to scream and snatch her hand back, but she did not—clenching her teeth and uttering not a sound. She heard a muted groan from the entire class.

Gritting her teeth, Rasha told herself, 'I won't cry—I'll die before I cry. I won't cry, won't cry, won't cry . . .'

She kept her hand outstretched, and the teacher brought his cane down on it again. Once again there was a crack, and once again the world turned black with pain.

Suddenly each of the students in the class stood up, all of them leaning forward, not saying a word. But their eyes bored into Razzak Sir. He was taken aback. He had raised the cane but, instead of bringing it down again, he put it away slowly, saying, 'What is it?'

No one spoke. He shouted, 'WHAT IS IT?' His voice must have sounded hollow even to his own ears. Gulping, he said, 'Why are all of you standing? Sit down!'

Now the students sat down slowly, but Rasha remained on her feet. Her hand was still outstretched. The message was clear—*you can cane me more if you like, I am not afraid.*

Razzak Sir looked around the classroom and then left with his chalk, duster and cane.

Rasha had been standing with a stone face all this time. As soon as the teacher left, she bowed her head and broke down in tears.

Something seemed to have happened to the entire class. Everyone rushed towards her from wherever they were. Even a few days ago, the boys in this class didn't talk to the girls, but something changed in an instant. A rough-looking boy stroked Rasha's head, saying, 'Don't cry. Don't cry, by the Lord.'

One of the boys raced away, wetting his handkerchief under the tap and pressing it softly against Rasha's palm. Two scarlet streaks had appeared on it by now. Another boy fanned her with a notebook and a third patted her shoulder. When Rasha looked up, tears were still streaming from her eyes. Sanjida tried to wipe them but Rasha did it herself. The boy whose merciless thrashing at the teacher's hands had made Rasha leap up in protest, threw his arms up and said disbelievingly, 'What have you done? We're used to being beaten up, but why you? *Why you?*'

A smallish boy with a calm face ground his teeth, saying, 'I'll kill him. I'll kill this man!'

Wiping her eyes, Rasha said quietly, 'It's OK. Everything's OK. I'm all right. Don't worry.'

The boys and girls surrounded Rasha, unsure of what to do.

As Rasha was going back home with the others in the evening, one of the shy boys from her class came up to her, saying softly, 'Rasha!'

'What?' asked Rasha.

'Yo-you . . . I mean . . . y-you . . .'

'Me?'

'Will you leave this school now?'

'No. Where will I go?'

'Don't leave, all right? All of us are with you.'

'I know,' said Rasha.

Rasha did know now that this incident had got the entire class to rally around her. It was the most terrible incident in her life but it had brought her close to every single student in her class.

Taught a Lesson—and What a Lesson!

Red welts had appeared on Rasha's palm from Razzak Sir's caning, which meant that she had to be very careful for the next few days to keep her grandmother from seeing them. Of course, her grandmother didn't take anything very seriously. So it was possible that she would not have asked about it even if it had caught her eye. Still, Rasha wasn't taking any chances. If her grandmother asked, Rasha would have to disclose everything—which she simply did not want to do.

All her classmates began to look at Rasha in a new light after the caning incident, but there was a big change in the behaviour of one of the boys in particular—a shy boy named Ratan. On the day of the incident, he had asked her whether she would leave school. Rasha noticed that he now hovered near her all the time, as though he wanted to tell her something.

Eventually, Rasha confronted him, 'Is there something you want to say?'

Nervous, Ratan lowered his voice. 'Yes.'

'What is it? Tell me.'

'I can't say it here.'

'Why not?'

'Everyone will hear!'

'So what?' asked Rasha in surprise.

Ratan shook his head. 'No, they mustn't!'

'When will you tell me then?'

'When you're on your way home. On the road.'

'Fine.'

As Rasha was walking home that evening with Jainab, Jitu and Moti, Ratan suddenly popped out of thin air at a particularly secluded spot. Looking around furtively, he whispered, 'Listen, Rasha.'

Rasha stopped, as did the rest.

With a mysterious air, Ratan said, 'Just you—tell the others to leave.'

'Why should they leave?' said Rasha. 'Let them wait.'

'All right, but far away.'

Rasha told Jainab, 'Walk up to the bridge and wait for me. I'll be there as soon as I've spoken to Ratan.'

Giving Ratan a deeply suspicious glare, Jainab looked at Rasha again before walking on ahead.

'All right, tell me now,' Rasha said to Ratan.

'You won't tell anyone, will you?'

'How can I promise that till I know what it is?' Rasha said a little impatiently. 'You have to tell me first!'

'An uncle of mine lives in London.'

Rasha looked at Ratan in astonishment. So much secrecy just to tell her his uncle lived in London?

'He's visiting us. He has three or four mobile phones.'

Rasha waited patiently for Ratan to finish the story of his uncle so that he'd get to the point. 'I asked my uncle, "Will you give me a mobile phone?"' said Ratan. '"You're a child," he said, "What will you do with a mobile phone? I'll buy you one when you grow up."'

Ratan paused and looked at Rasha with his eyes wide. Rasha wasn't sure what to say; she began to suspect Ratan of being a little strange—was he just going to keep telling her the story of his uncle's mobile phone?

That was precisely what happened. Ratan said, 'I told him, "Will you give me the phone with which I can take pictures? I want to take some pictures." He said, "You won't lose it? It's an expensive phone." I said, "No, I won't."'

Ratan stopped again, looking at Rasha as though he expected her to say something this time. But she didn't—she was waiting impatiently for the story to end. Ratan was in no hurry.

He said, 'It's a *very* expensive phone—it can take pictures and videos too. I've taken lots of photos and videos with it.'

Unable to contain herself any more, Rasha said, 'Good for you! Take more photos, more videos. I'm going!'

'Just wait till you find out what I did. I brought my uncle's phone to school one day, without telling anyone! The boys would just grab it if they knew—clamouring to have their pictures taken. It could fall from someone's hands and break. So I didn't show it to *anyone*!'

At the end of her tether by now, Rasha said, 'I live a long way from here, Ratan. It takes me hours to get home. Finish your phone story now and I'll listen to the rest tomorrow. I have to go!'

Ratan appeared dejected. 'You have to go?'

'Yes.'

'You don't want to see the video I shot in school?'

'Tomorrow.'

'Just watch a bit.'

Fishing an expensive mobile phone out of his pocket, Ratan began to press its buttons. Suddenly an angry roar was heard from the phone. Rasha looked at it curiously, to discover Razzak Sir rushing forward with a cane, using it on a student till he was flat on the floor. Then Rasha heard herself screaming sharply, '*Sir!*'

Stunned, Rasha asked, 'You made a video of the whole thing?'

Ratan replied gravely, '*The whole thing*. A first-class video! No one even saw me.'

'Show me, show me . . .'

Ratan handed her the phone, which now showed Razzak Sir dancing with a violent expression on his face. After exchanging a couple of words with Rasha, his cane flashed down on her palm. Unable to bear the sight, Rasha closed her eyes in a sort of terror. The teacher's brutal invectives streamed from the phone.

'My uncle is going back to London,' said Ratan.

'Will he take the phone with him?' asked Rasha.

'Yes.'

'We have to keep a copy of this video! It's vital for us.'

'That's why I wanted to talk to you in private,' explained Ratan.

'Why didn't you tell me earlier?' said Rasha. 'The next time you have something important to say, come straight to the point instead of beating about the bush. All right?'

'When did I beat about the bush?' asked Ratan, sounding injured. 'I came right to the point.'

'You did not.'

'Did too.'

'Never mind—there's no point arguing about this now. Tell me how we can get a copy of this.'

'Should I ask my uncle?'

'No way. Asking grown-ups just leads to trouble. Is there a computer shop in the market?'

'There is!'

'We have to get them to copy this on to a CD for us.'

'What's a CD?'

'I can't teach you now! Bring this phone to school tomorrow, all right? We'll take it to the market in the afternoon and copy the video.'

'All right.'

'Don't tell anyone.'

'I won't.'

'Keep it a secret.'

Making a face, Ratan said, 'That's exactly what *I* wanted to do—*you're* the one who wanted to talk in front of everyone!'

The next afternoon, the video was copied from the phone on to two CDs. Rasha put the discs away carefully—they were going to soon prove useful. She would discuss this with Jahanara Madam the next time she spoke to her. She would be upset when she'd hear that Rasha had been caned this way—but nothing could be done about that. There had to be a law against beating children in school, under which Razzak Sir could be punished. He needed to be taught a lesson but who was going to do it?

However, a chance to do this suddenly appeared. Rasha herself hadn't imagined that such a spectacular opportunity would present itself so soon.

At the morning assembly one day, the headmaster announced, 'I have some good news for all of you.'

Whenever teachers said that there was good news, it almost always turned out to be nothing of the sort. A few days earlier too the headmaster had said that he'd had good news for them—an MP would be visiting. All the children would have to welcome him by lining the road, holding tiny flags. From morning till late into the afternoon, the students had waited with their flags, with the sun blazing overhead. Everyone had been bathed in sweat. Eventually the MP had indeed turned up, a garland around his neck, surrounded by people. Fat and dark, he had walked past them without casting a single glance at the multitudes of schoolchildren lined up on either side of the road.

So this time when the headmaster said that there was good news, everyone looked at him apprehensively.

'How many of you have heard of computers?' asked the headmaster.

Almost everyone raised their hands. 'How many of you have *seen* a computer?' he asked.

This time all the hands went down, except Rasha's. But, noticing that she was the only one, she quickly lowered her hand too.

The headmaster said, 'In the developed world, every home has a computer. We are very unfortunate in not even being able to display computers to our students. But your days of deprivation are about to end! You will be delighted to know that the Ministry of Education is giving computers to every school in the country! And, under this programme, our school is about to get a computer too.'

As soon as he stopped, the children shouted with joy. This was genuinely good news, not the adulterated kind.

The headmaster continued, 'But there's something that everyone *must* remember. The computer is not like a television set, for which all you have to do is press a switch for the program to start, and the singing and dancing to begin. The computer is a very delicate machine. You must learn how to use it. Experts program computers—they use computers to write emails, to paint, to explore the Internet. Does everyone understand?'

Most of the students had no idea what the headmaster was saying but they all nodded. The headmaster went on, 'We want every student at our Ahad Ali High School to use computers some day!'

Once again the children cheered. The headmaster was pleased at their exuberance.

Smiling, he said, 'Our science teacher, Razzak Sahib, will go to Dhaka next week to be trained to use a computer. Then, people from Dhaka will come to install a computer in our school. We will be able to tell everyone that our school does not lag behind when it comes to information technology!' The headmaster raised a fist in the air and shook it in the manner of an orator.

There were cries of joy from the students again. Only Rasha sighed instead of cheering. A single computer for several hundred students, and Razzak Sir in charge! None of the children would even be allowed to *touch* the computer, let alone use it, Rasha thought to herself. The only good news was that Razzak Sir would be in Dhaka for a week. *That* would be a happy time for the students for they would not be caned.

There was great excitement in school through the next week. Lime was stirred into buckets of water and an attempt was made to whitewash the walls. The outcome was horrifying—patches of stark white here and there made the school look unfamiliar. The students were made to weed the fields and clean the classrooms.

On the day before the computer was to be installed, the headmaster showered more advice on the students. 'All of you must dress in clean clothes. I'm warning you—*no one must be barefoot, everyone should be in shoes or sandals*. Oil your hair and comb it. If the guests from Dhaka ask a question, answer pleasantly, using perfect grammar. No one must talk or cause a disturbance during the event. Pay attention to whatever is said. Remember—if you can create a good impression, we might get more computers in the future.'

As Rasha was about to leave for school the next day, on a whim she took the CD with Ratan's video, along with her.

When she arrived in school, she discovered a frenzy of activity. All the benches had been taken out of the classrooms and set out in the middle of the courtyard. A table and many chairs had been laid out in the veranda. Towels had been draped over the backs of the chairs, while the table was covered with a white cloth. A microphone stood on one side and two large speakers had been set up. Several CDs were arranged next to the computer. A vase adorned the table, with shiny plastic flowers in it.

At the back of the veranda stood a large white screen, with a video projector on a small table in front of it. The headmaster was rushing about, with a tie around his neck. Razzak Sir was dressed in a crisp safari suit. The other teachers were also dressed well.

With all the benches outside, there was nowhere to sit in the classrooms. So the students sat on the benches in the yard in silence. Someone turned the microphone on to test it, saying, 'Hello . . . testing one-two-three-four, one-two-three-four.'

Rasha spotted a number of bouquets in a corner. The headmaster seemed to suddenly remember something and rushed towards the students. 'We forgot to decide who will offer the bouquets! Where are the girls from class nine?'

It turned out that they were two girls short in class nine. So two girls from class eight were added to the group. Sanjida and Rasha. Shutting her eyes, Rasha turned her face towards the sky and whispered, 'Thank you, Allah. Thank you very much!'

The guests were very late and everyone grew impatient, but not Rasha. She waited calmly, so that no one would know her heart was thumping like a moving train.

Eventually the guests arrived—two cars pulled up on the school field, followed by a police vehicle. When they emerged from the car, the headmaster led them to the stage, visibly overcome with gratitude at their presence. Despite the heat, one of the guests was in a suit and tie, the very sight of which made Rasha feel warm. One of the others, in a police uniform, was unwilling to sit on the stage but the headmaster insisted. The guests were in a great hurry, for they would have to visit another school too. So the ceremonies began at once.

Razzak Sir behaved like the master of ceremonies. He heaped praises on the guests in a theatrical manner, almost foaming at the mouth in expressing his gratitude at the fact that the Superintendent of Police and the District Commissioner Sahib had wasted their valuable time by visiting a school as insignificant as this one. Then the girls were called on stage to present the flowers. Rasha took the CD out of the book she had hidden it in, holding her hand behind her back so that no one could see it. Collecting her bouquet, she concealed the CD behind it. One by one, the girls went forward to present the bouquets. When Rasha's turn came, she quietly put the CD on top of the pile of CDs as she was passing the table. The gentleman in the suit accepted the bouquet from her, saying something which she could not hear clearly because her heart was beating furiously.

Returning to her seat, Rasha shut her eyes again and turned her face up to the sky, muttering, 'I've done my bit, *Khuda*. Please do the rest.'

The guests were supposed to give a speech but the man in the suit did not want to get into all this. He signalled a younger person sitting in front, who jumped to his feet and began to speak into the microphone. He seemed jovial and spoke well, so everyone listened to him with interest.

'Most of the people gathered here are children,' he said. 'Children cannot stand speeches so there will be no speeches today! We will go straight to the best part of the day. Does anyone know what the best thing today is?'

'THE COMPUTER!' screamed everyone in unison.

'Very good,' the young speaker said, smiling. 'Tell me what you can do on a computer.'

Now the students were silent. One of them said hesitantly, 'We can watch Hindi movies.'

The speaker laughed. 'You could've just mentioned watching films. But Hindi films! Not that I blame you—you must have seen them screening Hindi films on the computer at some shop or the other? All right, what else?'

'We can write letters,' said another student.

'Very good! Letters. What else?'

'Paint,' said another.

'And?'

'Play games.'

'What else?'

Rasha wanted to list dozens of things that could be done on a computer, but she kept quiet.

Having heard out the students and their suggestions, the speaker finally said, 'All the things you have mentioned can be done on a computer—but that's not all. There's a *lot* more you can do. Instead of lecturing you, let me show you. All right?'

'All right!' the students shouted.

The young man picked up the CDs lying next to the computer, and Rasha's heart jumped into her mouth.

The man said, 'I've brought several CDs for you. Some of these are games, some encyclopedias, some are guides to scientific experiments, some are music, some are painting programs. I'll show them to you one by one. Which one do you want to see first?'

'The games, the games!' yelled most of the students.

Running his eyes over the CDs, the speaker stopped suddenly. Holding up the one Rasha had slipped into the pile, he said, 'How interesting, a new CD! Someone has left it here. It says, "Our School". Which means someone has made a CD about your school! Let's start with this one. Let's find out what your school is like.'

The headmaster looked bewildered at this. He asked Razzak Sir a question in a low voice, who said that he knew nothing about it. Both of them looked worried.

Inserting the CD in the computer, the man with the mic said, 'Computer monitors are small, visible to only one person at a time. Today, we have a projector and a large screen here so that all of us can see whatever's displayed on the computer screen. Together!'

Rasha stopped breathing, her eyes closed in anticipation. And at once Razzak Sir's distorted screams emerged from the speakers, *'Swine, pig!'*

The guests on the stage, the sirs and madams seated in front, and the hundreds of children on the benches all jumped in their seats in unison. Everyone looked at the screen in astonishment, where Razzak Sir could be seen with a cane in his hand, snarling at a student. *'I will kill you. I will take your skin off with this cane, I will beat you to a pulp!'*

Everyone watched as Razzak Sir pounced on a boy with his cane, thrashing him mercilessly. No one would have believed it if they hadn't seen it with their own eyes. The guests, the teachers and the students all stared in disbelief at this inhuman scene.

Rasha was looking at Razzak Sir, who jumped to his feet and tried to shut the computer down.

'What's going on here?' he screamed.

No one listened. The young man, who was standing near the computer, shoved him aside and kept looking at the screen. Everyone saw Razzak Sir beating up the boy, who tried to protect himself by raising his arm, at which the teacher grew even more furious, grabbed him by his hair and forced him to almost lie down on a bench while he continued to beat him. The student's stricken cries matched the whistling of the cane.

Suddenly Rasha's sharp cry was heard from the speakers. *'Sir!'*

The audience was startled once again. On the screen, Razzak Sir was seen turning around. He looked like a wild beast.

'Who was that?' he could be heard asking violently.

Rasha was not visible, but her voice could be heard. *'Me, Sir.'*

'What is it?'

'You cannot beat him like this.'

The audience tried to identify the girl who had been so bold, who had dared to speak up this way. She could not be seen on the screen, just Razzak Sir was visible. It was only when he went up to Rasha that she was seen for the first time. From the back, but clearly.

Razzak Sir rushed up to the stage again and tried to shut the computer down, but to no avail. The speaker pushed him away so hard that he barely managed to save himself from falling off the stage.

Everyone watched Razzak Sir bringing his cane down repeatedly on Rasha's palm. Everyone watched the students in the class rise to their feet, watched Razzak Sir stop abruptly and race out of the classroom, watched Rasha break down in tears and the other students rush to her. That's when the video ended and the screen turned black.

No one spoke. They sat in their places like blocks of stone. Rasha saw the man in the suit surreptitiously wiping his eye.

The headmaster remained seated, his eyes on the floor. Only Razzak Sir was seen trying to say something but not succeeding, his face robbed of colour and looking like an ugly, giant insect.

The man in the suit said something, but without a mic, so no one could hear him. The young man took the microphone off its stand and handed it to him. The older man said, 'We are giving computers to schools, making big speeches—but what's the use? We're handing over our children to demons. These demons are killing our children and we don't even know it. What's the use then? *What's the use?*'

Turning to the headmaster, the man in the suit said, 'Headmaster Sahib, don't you know that your students are caned this way? What sort of headmaster are you? How can we entrust you with the responsibility of our children? *How?*'

The headmaster muttered something, his eyes still on the floor. The man in the suit then told the man in the police uniform, 'Arrest this demon, SP Sahib. Book him! If he gets out of jail in less than fourteen year—'

Rushing up to the man in the suit like a madman, Razzak Sir tried to grab his legs and broke down in tears. He shouted at Razzak Sir so loudly that the entire school trembled. 'Don't you dare! I'll kill you if you touch me!'

Looking behind him, he said, 'Take him away. Remove him from the premises. I don't want any more drama.'

Several people led Razzak Sir away. The man in the suit had been seated all this while. Now he took the microphone and stood up, then walked to the front of the gathering.

After a pause, he said, 'Do you know who the most respected people in the world are? Teachers. A teacher must never be dishonoured. But if a teacher dishonours *himself*, there's nothing we can do. We are saddened—but there's nothing we can do. Boys and girls, I am *deeply* saddened today. If there is one incident like this here, then there must be many others at the other 80,000 schools in our country. Perhaps a teacher is beating up a boy or a girl somewhere in one of these schools at this very moment! Can you imagine? We have taken the responsibility of imparting education in our country. Will the Lord forgive us? I doubt it. Khuda will not forgive us.'

Drawing a deep breath, he carried on, 'It is true that I am saddened but my heart is also full because of what I have observed. Such a young girl but how courageous—how she stood up for her friend, how she did not back down although she was beaten. I don't know if you are here, my girl. But, if you are, I salute you!' He raised his hand in a salute.

The students applauded, some of them trying to get Rasha to stand up. But she refused, remaining seated with her eyes on the ground.

The man in the suit said, 'When *you* grow up and take responsibility for our nation, no child will suffer in a classroom. All right?'

'All right,' the students nodded.

'Promise me!'

Everyone promised.

Now the young man by the computer came up to the man in the suit and said something. Making some calculations, he nodded and said something more, and nodded again, after which the two of them appeared to come to an agreement.

Taking the mic, the younger man said, 'I was given the responsibility of demonstrating a computer to you, of explaining the use of information technology. But what did I see? I saw that *you* understand computers much better than I do! You used information technology to expose to us a serious wrongdoing. So I have nothing to teach you. On the contrary, I have learnt a great deal from you today.'

The students clapped happily.

The person said, 'I spoke to sir just now. I told him, seeing how well the children here can use a computer, "What's the use of giving them just one? They must get more computers." How many do you want?'

'Ten!' shouted one of the students from the front row.

'Only ten? We will give you thirty computers. Thirty!'

His voice was drowned in cheers. The students rose to their feet, jumping up and down. When they had quieted down, he added, 'We can see that you have no space here for so many computers, so sir has said that he will have a room constructed in that corner. That will be your computer laboratory!'

Now even the teachers began to jump up and down with joy.

Rasha alone sat quietly. She felt as though she wasn't a little girl any more. Jumping up and down no longer befitted her.

Only a smile appeared on her face, widening slowly.

Motku Mian and Others

Rasha stood chest-deep in the pond—near the steps leading out of the water—with Jainab on the other end. Jainab had taken the responsibility of teaching Rasha how to swim. They had been practising for the past few days.

'Dip your head under the water and come up to me,' Jainab told Rasha.

'It's easy for *you* to say that,' said Rasha. 'But how am *I* supposed to do it? Won't the water get into my nose and mouth?'

'No, it won't,' assured Jainab. 'It's the easiest to learn how to swim with your head underwater. Once you've learnt this, you can learn how to hold your head above water too. Come!'

'I'm scared,' said Rasha.

'Scared of what?' asked Jainab. 'I'm right here. Just come.'

'Still—I'm scared,' whined Rasha.

'You're such a coward!' said Jainab. 'All right, I'll come up to you. Then you can hold on to me.'

Clutching Jainab, Rasha splashed about with her arms and legs, trying to swim. But whatever the outcome was, it certainly couldn't be called swimming.

Jitu turned up at this point. He observed Rasha's flailing limbs and unsuccessful attempts at swimming with great attention for some time, before breaking into giggles.

Rasha stopped splashing. 'What is it? What's that show of teeth for?'

'If you keep trying to swim like this for a few more days, all the water in the pond will end up on land!'

'*Very funny*. You must have learnt to swim the same way.'

Jitu Mian shook his head. 'Uh-uh. It took *me* just one hour to learn.'

'Don't lie! No one can learn how to swim in an hour.'

'I did.'

'*How?*'

'My father threw me into the water.'

'*What did he do?*'

'He threw me into the water.'

'You didn't know how to swim and yet your father threw you into the water?' Rasha asked in consternation.

'Yes.'

'And then?'

'I swallowed water and was drowning. When I was almost dead, my father held my head above the water. Just as I had recovered after a few breaths of air, he threw me back in.'

'Really?'

'Yes. I tried to float to save my life. When I couldn't—when I had water in my mouth and nose—my father held my head above the water again, giving me time to take a couple of breaths, before pushing me back under.'

'Don't you lie to me!'

'I swear by the Lord, I'm not lying. After a while, I *did* learn how to float. Within an hour.'

'That's horrible,' said Rasha, exhaling. 'Your father should be sued for child abuse!'

Giggling, Jitu said, 'You're stranger, Rashapu. Totally stranger!'

'Very well then, I *am* stranger,' declared Rasha. 'Don't disturb me.'

Watching Rasha's attempts to swim for some more time, Jitu shook his head hopelessly. 'You won't be able to teach Rashapu how to swim, Jainab Bubu,' he said. 'Let *me* try—*I'll* teach her.'

'How will you teach me?' Rasha asked.

'I'll push you into the water! You'll swallow some and then swim to shore.'

'I'll kill you, Jitu!' Rasha screamed. 'I won't spare you alive. Don't you dare come anywhere near me—don't come within a hundred miles of me!'

Jitu enjoyed Rasha's terror, giggling uncontrollably. Then he took off his shirt and plunged into the water, disappearing. He surfaced much later in the middle of the pond with a splash. He didn't even seem to remember he was in water. He could float on the surface without moving a limb. No one knows—maybe he could even sleep that way. Rasha stared at Jitu in envy.

Having sunk underwater every single time, no matter how hard she tried, Rasha had more or less given up on swimming when she suddenly found herself staying afloat for some time.

'There, you've got it,' said Jainab happily. 'Stop worrying, you'll learn how to swim now!'

'Really?' Rasha asked, wide-eyed.

'Really.'

What Jainab said turned out to be true. For the past few days, Rasha had not managed to stay afloat despite her best efforts—but she could do it now. She didn't understand *how* it was possible. Here was a person who couldn't float for a moment, sinking like a marble every time. And then the same person could float so effortlessly, you couldn't make them sink even if you tried! Just as she had seen Jitu float without moving a finger.

Rasha couldn't be persuaded to get out of the water for the next few days. She would stay in so long that her skin would become wrinkled like raisins. By the time she'd come out, her eyes would be flaming red and her vision, blurred. When she'd sit down to eat, she'd discover herself famished and would eat a huge amount of rice every day. When she had arrived here, her skin used to have a pallor like blades of grass smothered under a brick. Now her complexion was a coppery brown. There was a new liveliness about her. Rasha was surprised when she looked at herself in the mirror. She walked three miles to school and three miles home, and swam across the pond with ease. She felt a certain power, the sort of physical power she had never felt before.

After she had learnt how to swim, Rasha turned her attention to climbing trees. This time, Moti was her tutor. Rasha discovered that climbing was not as difficult as swimming. In fact, it was far easier, needing only a combination of courage and confidence. Jainab had been very keen on teaching Rasha how to swim but it turned out that she was far less interested in Rasha's tree-climbing. With guava and mango trees conquered, Rasha tried to master coconut trees. But Jainab put her foot down now.

'You're overdoing it, Rasha,' she said.

'What am I overdoing?'

'Climbing coconut trees!'

'How? How am I overdoing it?'

'There's a limit to everything. Some things are meant to be done only by men and some only by women.'

Rasha shook her head. 'That's not true. A woman can do everything a man can.'

'Then go ask a woman to shave.'

Rasha's face hardened. 'That's different. How can women shave when they don't have beards?'

'It's not different at all. Some things are just not right for women—like climbing a coconut tree.'

'*Why not?*'

'Think about it. There you are, climbing a coconut tree like a monkey, with your legs wrapped around the trunk. Do you think it's a pretty sight? It's not; it's ugly.'

Rasha wasn't one to give up easily, but Jainab tried a different tack. She said that if Moti continued to give lessons to Rasha on tree-climbing, she would break his leg. Jainab was a quiet sort but those who knew her were in awe of her. So Moti backed out, and Rasha couldn't complete her lessons.

Even though Moti couldn't teach her how to climb a tree, he did teach her how to trap herons. He arranged the set-up himself. It started with a forked branch from a tree, which he cut to about a foot and half in length. Then he embedded a spoke from a cycle-wheel at the forked end of the branch. A loop was made with strong thread at the head of the spoke, and some food was placed there as bait. As soon as a heron pecked at it, the loop tightened around its neck. Rasha observed all this with great interest but when she saw the bait, her stomach churned. It was a fat cockroach, a living one.

Rasha accompanied Moti to the rice fields to set the trap and then waited in the shade of a banyan tree nearby. Moti had said that it wasn't easy to trap a heron, that it might take three or four days. But luck was on Rasha's side and a heron was caught the very first day. When it was writhing in the trap, Rasha ran up to it.

Removing the noose and holding the heron firmly, Moti told her, 'Be very careful of herons.'

'Why?'

'A heron can peck your eyes out!'

The bird looked so placid and innocent in Moti's grip that Rasha could not believe that it was capable of pecking anyone's eyes out. But still she was wary. Handing her the heron, Moti explained to her what she would have to do to keep it—what to feed it twice a day and so on.

Rasha put the heron under a large upturned basket at home. She had given it some food following Moti's advice, but it didn't even touch it. It only paced up and down restlessly, trying to escape even though it knew it couldn't. You could tell from people's expressions when they were upset, but there was no such sign among birds. The heron's face did not reveal his unhappiness, but its constant pacing conveyed it clearly. Maybe the heron was a mother, who had been foraging for food for her children back home. Perhaps the children were waiting for their mother. All these thoughts made Rasha sad. In the afternoon, she reached into the basket and, bringing the heron out, stroked its back, whispering, 'I'm setting you free, go back to your babies. Take a couple of fish for them. All right? And listen, can you learn to be well behaved? How can you peck out people's eyes? I don't want to hear that again . . .'

Then Rasha threw the heron up in the air and at once it fluttered its wings, rose upwards, circled overhead once and flew away towards the rice fields. Rasha was certain that the circle was to say thank you.

From Jitu, Rasha learnt how to fish with a rod. Fishing needed bait, and Jitu felt that what fish liked best were earthworms. Rasha's stomach turned but still she followed Jitu. Apparently earthworms were to be found in the tiny mounds of earth in damp areas. As soon as Jitu plunged a spade into one of them, innumerable earthworms of different sizes slithered out. Piling some soil on a large leaf, Jitu let loose a few fat worms on it. Then he left with Rasha, carrying a sack for their fishing rods and the fish that they would catch. Taking her to a part of the village with a stagnant pond in the shade of some trees, Jitu sat down with his fishing rod. Fixing the bait to the hook at the end of the rod was a violent affair. To do so, Jitu tore off a portion of the worm with his nails and attached it to the hook. Rasha saw in surprise that both the severed sections were still wriggling. So strange! So creepy!

Holding out the fishing rod, Jitu stared at the float in the water. When it started moving, Jitu said, 'The fish are nibbling!'

'Should we pull out the rod now?'

'No, not yet. Only after the float has sunk.'

Rasha kept waiting but it just didn't sink. Eventually Jitu did pull the rod out, only to find that the fish had eaten the bait and escaped.

'Fish are very clever,' Jitu said. 'They swallow the bait but not the hook.'

'What will we do now?' Rasha asked.

'Fix fresh bait to the hook.'

'*Me?*'

'Who else? You expect to do the fishing while someone else fixes the bait?'

Rasha had never imagined that she would tear off a portion of a fat, red earthworm with her nails, or that it would wriggle in her hands while she calmly impaled it on a hook—without shrieking. But that was just what she did, and she didn't even throw up!

This time, the float began to move soon after the line was thrown into the water and then sank suddenly. At once Rasha whipped the rod out of the water. And there it was—how amazing—a wriggling, plump fish. Black as the night, impaled on the hook.

'What an enormous *maagur*!' Jitu shouted in joy.

'Is this a maagur? Looks like a snake's nephew.'

'What nonsense! Why should it be a snake's nephew? It's a maagur. Very tasty!'

The fish was thrashing about. Jitu took the hook out of its mouth and put the fish in the sack. Rasha gazed at it in wonder—the first fish she had caught in her life! The maagur was staring back at her with bulbous eyes.

'You know what I think?' Rasha said.

'What?'

'It isn't really a fish.'

'What is it then?'

'It's actually a princess.'

'*A princess?*'

'Yes. A sage cursed her and turned her into a fish before depositing her at the bottom of this pond.'

A shadow of fear appeared in Jitu Mian's eyes. 'Is that what you think?' he mumbled uneasily.

'Yes, don't you see how it's looking at us? Obviously it's saying, "Let me go, please let me go. When my curse wears off, I'll turn back into a princess. But if you eat me up, I'll never be a princess again!"'

Rasha poured so much emotion into her words that Jitu was confused. 'What do we do now?' he asked. 'Let it go?'

'Yes, let's do that!'

So Rasha and Jitu released the cursed princess back into the stagnant pond. Of course, whenever Jitu told the story afterwards, he had the licence to make the fish as big as he wanted it to be. Depending on whom he was telling the story to, the fish kept growing in size.

Rasha learnt not only how to swim, climb trees, trap birds and catch fish, but also to identify all the trees in the village. She had no fixed tutor on this subject—more or less everyone was her instructor. For instance, Nani would pluck some leaves and vines from one corner of the bank of the pond and cook them—apparently this was *kolmishaak*. Or Jainab would point to the white flowers and the fruit of a low tree, saying, 'Be very careful of these. These are thorn apples—anything from this tree is poisonous.'

Rasha took care to identify the tree. 'If I ever want to die, all I'll have to do is eat this fruit, right?'

'What a thing to say!' Jainab shook her head. 'Why do you want to die?'

Drawing Rasha's attention to an innocuous-looking plant, Jitu said, 'If you want to teach anyone a lesson,

Rashapu, just rub these leaves on their shoulders. Then sit back and watch the fun!'

'What will happen?'

'They will kill themselves scratching the itch!' Jitu must have been savouring the scene he had conjured up before his eyes, because his face lit up with happiness.

Frowning, Rasha asked, 'But won't *my* fingers itch when I pluck it?'

'You must hold it very carefully, at the base. Just make sure not to touch the leaves.'

And so Rasha's knowledge of village life grew. Not that all of it would prove useful, but then knowledge couldn't be thrown away either. It didn't matter whether she wanted to know these things or not—thousands of useful as well as useless bits of information began to gather in her head.

But it wasn't as though Rasha was the only one learning—sometimes she shared what *she* knew with the others. Take the business of the leech, for instance.

On her way back from school one day, Rasha felt an itch on her ankle. Rubbing the spot with her other foot, she continued walking. When they were almost home, Moti suddenly screamed, 'Rasha Bubu! Wait!'

'What's the matter?' Rasha asked in alarm.

'A leech!'

'*Leech?*' It was Rasha's turn to scream. 'Where?'

'On your ankle!'

Rasha began to hop with terror, not knowing what she should do.

'Don't move, don't move,' Moti told her.

Rasha was about to have a heart attack but she tried to stand still, while everyone else closed in on her ankle. She saw an oily, slippery, black creature clinging to her skin. Moti tried to pull it off but the more he pulled, the more it stretched like a rubber band, without letting go. But after several attempts, Moti finally managed to prise it off. He was about to grind it underfoot when Rasha stopped him. 'Wait, wait!'

'What is it?'

'Don't kill the leech.'

'Why not?'

'I need it.'

'For what?'

Rasha examined her ankle. The spot where the leech had attacked her was bleeding—she knew it would bleed for a while. She had read on the Internet that there was something in the saliva of leeches that numbed sensation—which was why she had felt no pain, only a slight itch at first. There was something else in its saliva that prevented the blood from clotting, which was why the leech could drink it so easily. The worm was bloated from all the blood it had consumed. It tried to slither away slowly.

'We have to catch this leech!' declared Rasha.

'What will you do with it?'

'I'll keep it as a pet.'

'*A pet?* Ugh!' exclaimed Jainab.

'Leeches are extraordinary creatures,' Rasha explained. 'I've read that once a leech has drunk its fill of blood, it can go without food for two years!'

'Impossible!'

'It's true. I'm sure that this rascal has had its fill of my blood—now I want to see how long it can fast!'

Jitu's eyes brightened. 'You're really going to keep it as a pet?'

'Yes, I'll fill a bottle with water and put the leech in it. You'll see . . . it'll stay alive for at least a year. And another thing!'

'What?'

'Leeches can sense air pressure. So you'll see this leech come out of the water whenever a storm is brewing.'

'I don't believe you.'

'*Honest!*' said Rasha. 'I read it on the Net.'

So the leech was brought home carefully and released into a plastic bottle filled with water. It began to swim around happily.

'We have to give the leech a name,' said Rasha.

'What name?' Jitu Mian's face shone with pleasure.

'Got any ideas?'

'It drank your blood. Call it Bloodsucker!'

'No, that's too much of a mouthful. Something simpler.'

'It's so fat with blood . . . Fatka Mian? Or Motku Mian—the Fat Man.'

Rasha said, 'Motku Mian is a good name. Let's name it Motku Mian! All right?'

Everyone nodded.

But Nani wrinkled her nose in disgust. '*A leech?* A leech in a bottle? Does nothing disgust you, Rasha?'

'Nani, its name is Motku Mian!'

'A leech with a name!'

'Yes, Nani. It's grown fat on my blood, so it is Motku Mian.'

'Tell me right now what else you plan to keep as a pet! A snake? A frog? A scorpion?'

'Nothing else, Nani. This leech is actually a barometer—if it comes out of the water, there'll be a storm coming.'

Nani shook her head. 'There's no need to observe your leech to find out whether a storm is on its way. You only have to look at the sky!'

There wasn't a man or beast in the village who had not been bitten by a leech. So there should have been no particular curiosity about the creature, but still Motku Mian became popular. Anyone passing that way stopped to visit Motku Mian, who'd curl up peacefully in the water, completely unaware of the excitement he was generating.

But Motku Mian didn't let Rasha down. One afternoon, when it was very hot and the atmosphere, oppressive, Nani said, 'I don't like this sort of day.'

Rasha asked, 'Why, Nani? Why don't you like this sort of day?'

'Looks like a storm is brewing.'

At once Rasha fetched Motku Mian, who had indeed come out of the water. 'You're right, Nani,' said Rasha. 'See, Motku Mian has crawled out of the water! Looks like there really will be a storm today.'

Sure enough, a dark cloud appeared in a corner of the sky soon afterwards. And then the entire sky became overcast. Rasha stared at the darkened sky holding her breath—she had never seen such an angry and menacing sky before. Soon the heavens were cracked open by bolts of lightning, accompanied by rumbles of thunder. For a moment there was no wind at all, then suddenly there was a gust, sending leaves and bits of straw flying in the air. Dust covered everything. The cattle began to stampede, lowing at the top of their voices, and the birds soared in the air, calling loudly. Rasha stood outside, looking around. The gusts of wind made the familiar fields and trees look completely different, threatening to blow her away too.

Nani shouted, 'Come inside, Rasha! The storm's about to break.'

'Let me stay out, Nani? I want to get drenched in the rain.'

Nani looked at Rasha in wonder. 'What did you say?'

'I said I want to get drenched in the rain!'

Nani gazed at Rasha for a few moments before saying, 'All right.'

Rasha stood outside the house. First, a few fat drops of rain fell on her, then a few more, and then some more. Now it began to rain torrentially. Spreading her arms wide, Rasha turned her face up to the rain and began to dance. She felt as though she was a primitive woman in the forest, with no one for company except the birds, the animals, the plants and the trees. She was dancing and, along with her, all the animals and birds and trees were dancing too. Rasha sang as she danced, first softly, and then out loud.

Suddenly she heard someone calling, '*Rashapu, Rashapu* . . .'

Rasha turned around. Jitu, Moti, Jainab and the other children had also arrived, all drenched. Rasha laughed with joy. 'What fun!'

They couldn't hear one another over the sound of the rain but that made no difference. Everyone jumped in delight—dancing, singing songs without a beginning or an end.

Nani sat outside her room, watching. Her husband had been captured nearly forty years ago. He used to get drenched in the rain the same way. It had been raining exactly like this the day the razakars had taken him away.

Nani noticed that her hand was trembling. She felt her head begin to whirl; a sense of confusion overtook her. But Nani tried to sit still through all of this.

When Sanjida Was the Bride

Rasha and the other village children were in school earlier than usual that day. They normally travelled in a group. And it always seemed that either some of them missed breakfast, some others couldn't find their English notebooks, or someone would lose a button in a critical area of their pants which needed to be stitched back in place immediately. Sometimes all of them found themselves in two minds about whether to go to school or not. All told, there was a considerable waste of time every day, which was why preparations had to start early. Today, for some reason, no one was late. And so when they arrived at school, no one else was present. The office boy was only just unlocking the classrooms.

Rasha had just about settled down in the veranda, stretching her legs out comfortably, when she spotted a lanky boy approaching her hesitantly, looking apprehensive. He had the mark of a village boy written all over him.

After a few more furtive looks in different directions, he came up to ask Jitu, 'Which way to class eight?'

Jitu attempted to point towards the classroom.

'Why? What do you need to go to class eight for?' Rasha asked.

'A letter.'

'*A letter?* From whom?'

After a few more glances in every direction, the boy lowered his voice to answer, 'Sanjida.'

'Give it to me. I'm in class eight.'

'Really?'

'Of course.'

'Private letter. Sanjida said to take it to class eight. She named a girl, Khasha or Masha or something . . .'

'*Rasha?*' asked Rasha sternly.

'Oh yes, Rasha!'

'I'm Rasha. Give it to me.'

With a final look around him, the boy took a folded letter out of his breast pocket and handed it to Rasha. It said—

I'm in great trouble. They're forcing me to get married this afternoon. If you don't rescue me, I'll hang myself. —Sanjida

Rasha read the letter twice, and then whispered, '*Oh my god!*'

Jainab, who was standing next to her, asked, 'What's the matter?'

'They're forcing Sanjida to get married!'

Jainab sighed. 'It's the same story every time. They'll get me married by force too one day—take my word for it.'

'Never! You can't get a girl married till she's eighteen. It's illegal!'

Jainab smiled sarcastically. 'And who's going to find out that it's been done illegally?'

'*We'll* inform them.'

'Inform *whom*?'

'The police.'

'As if the police have nothing better to do. You really think that they will help you stop the wedding?'

This was true. The police were unlikely to be perturbed by her complaint. As Rasha bit her lip, wondering what to do, the lanky boy said, 'I'll go now.'

'Where will you go?'

'Back home. I came away without telling anyone. They'll suspect something is wrong if I don't go back.'

'Are you related to Sanjida?'

'I'm her cousin. Her mother's brother's son.'

'How's Sanjida?'

'Not well. She's crying constantly. So they've locked her in a room.'

Rasha sighed. 'What does the boy do, the one they're getting her married to?'

'*Boy?* You think they're getting her married to a boy? The wedding is with a grown-up man!'

'Same thing,' said Rasha impatiently. 'What does this *man* do?'

'Nothing. He has some land which he lives off.'

Rasha snorted. 'Is he educated?'

The boy tried to smile. '*Educated?* How would a villager be educated?'

'Not educated, doesn't do any work, but wants to get married?'

'Who doesn't want to get married?' said the boy indifferently.

Rasha glared at him without a word.

'I'll go now,' he said quickly.

'Wait, tell me where Sanjida lives. How far is it?'

'Not very far from here. In Gokulpur village. Her father's name is Mahtab Husain. Anyone in the village will show you the house if you ask.'

'What did you say the village is called? Gokulpur?'

'No, Gokulpur.'

'That's what I said. Gokulpur.'

'No, you're calling it Gokulpur. The name is actually Gokulpur.'

Rasha listened closely but found no difference in the two ways in which they were pronouncing the name. Giving up, she said, 'How do you get there?'

'Go south after the market.'

'I can't tell north from south. Do I turn right or left?'

The boy looked confused. Just as Rasha couldn't tell north from south, he couldn't tell right from left. After some thought he said, 'Left if you're going from the east. Right if you're going from the west.'

'I can't tell east and west either!' exhaled Rasha impatiently.

The boy said testily, 'Ask for the way to Sukhankandi when you get to the market . . .'

'Didn't you say Gokulpur a minute ago? It's Sukhankandi now?'

'Gokulpur is to the east of Sukhankandi.'

Rasha was in despair. 'Wait. I'll go with you.'

'*You?*' Jainab asked with a frown. 'You'll go? *Now?*'

'Of course. I have to!'

'What will you do?'

'I'll tell them that they cannot get Sanjida married now. That it's illegal to get a girl married before she turns eighteen.'

'You expect Sanjida's family to listen to you?'

'Why won't they?'

'Have you ever seen yourself in the mirror?'

'Why wouldn't I? Hundreds of times.'

'You haven't. If you had, you'd have known that you're *tina*! And a girl on top of that. No one will listen to you.'

'The word is *tiny*, not tina. And besides, I'm a person. Whether I'm a girl or not doesn't matter. Anyone can tell the truth—whether they're young or old or a man or a woman makes no difference.'

'All right. Don't blame me when Sanjida's family throws you out.'

'You don't think I'm going alone, do you?'

'Who will you take along with you?'

'You!'

'*Me?*'

'Yes. Let's go!'

Staring at Rasha, Jainab shook her head helplessly. 'The Lord alone knows what perils you'll lead me into one day.'

'Let's go find out where Sanjida lives,' said Rasha. 'Then the entire class will go and surround their house. We'll form a human chain! We'll go on a fast!'

'You have *no* idea what village people are like,' Jainab told her.

'So what if I don't? Let's go.'

'I'll come too,' said Jitu.

'No, you stay here,' said Rasha. 'You can come when I take the rest of the class. I'm writing a letter to them—you give it to them when they turn up. We'll go, locate the house and come back at once! We're leaving our books here, look after them.'

Scribbling a letter to her classmates, Rasha handed it to Jitu. He stood sadly with the letter, while Rasha set off with the lanky boy, accompanied by Jainab, who muttered, 'If they find out at home that I'm skipping school to run around in the countryside with you, I'll be in for trouble!'

'If you are, you are. We're going there to save Sanjida. Don't you remember that she said she'd kill herself if we can't rescue her?'

'That's true.' Jainab nodded.

Soon after they had left, Rasha realized that they had been wise to have accompanied the lanky boy. The strange route that he took convinced her that she would never have made it on her own. He had said that Sanjida lived close by, but she should have remembered that words like 'near' and 'far' held no meaning for rural people. Any place that you could walk to was considered near.

By the time they reached Sanjida's house, both Rasha and Jainab were covered in sweat. The lanky boy said, 'The groom's party seems to have arrived.'

Rasha was startled. '*They've arrived?* But Sanjida's letter said that the wedding was in the afternoon. It's still morning!'

'Village people don't distinguish between morning and afternoon,' explained Jainab. 'They only know the difference between day and night.'

'Oh my god! What if they force her to get married right away?'

Jainab looked grimly at Rasha without answering. Rasha stood there for a while, thinking. Then she exhaled loudly and told the lanky boy, 'Can you take me to Sanjida's father?'

'Are you crazy?' he said. 'You think I have two lives to spare? I can't take you to anyone. You can go on your own if you like.'

'Can you at least do this one thing for us then?' asked Rasha.

'What's that?'

'Don't tell anyone we're from Sanjida's school. All right?'

'All right.'

'Let's go,' Rasha told Jainab.

'Wait!'

'Now what?'

'Let me say a holy verse first.'

Uttering the words three times, Jainab blew on her own breast, followed by Rasha's. Then they entered Sanjida's home together.

Normally, a house hosting a wedding is abuzz with excitement, with signs of celebrations everywhere. But there was no trace of merriment here, and people milled about grimly. There weren't too many people anyway, nor any little children dressed up in finery rushing back and forth. No one realized that Rasha and Jainab were outsiders, each of the families assuming that they belonged to the other.

They discovered the groom's party as soon as they entered. The man who was to be married was as scrawny as a patient suffering from tuberculosis, with sunken cheeks and a sallow complexion. He was dressed in a traditional long, silk shirt, with a cap instead of a ceremonial turban on his head. There was a garland around his neck, the kind that is draped around a cow before sacrificing it. Rasha had never seen it adorn a human before. Several people of different ages sat around with sombre expressions.

A few old men were seated on chairs in the yard, discussing something in low voices. It looked as though it was a very serious matter. Rasha hovered nearby in order to eavesdrop.

A shrewd-looking person said, 'What do you mean, no motorcycle? Have you seen anyone get married without a motorcycle these days?'

An elderly man, possibly Sanjida's father, said apprehensively, 'How can I afford a motorcycle? I'm a poor man . . .'

'It's all very well for you to be a poor man, but our boy is respected in his village. When he returns home with his bride, everyone will ask him about the dowry. What shall we tell them?'

'But that is not what was agreed upon. When we'd finalized the marriage, you'd said that you didn't want anything! All you wanted was a pretty wife for your boy. My daughter is as lovely as a flower . . .'

The sly man said, 'Why would we even be here if she weren't beautiful?'

Rasha felt an urge to throttle him, but resisted. She walked away instead. She had never imagined that anyone could be so brazen. All this time she had been beset with anxiety, now anger was added to it. She had more or less decided to do something drastic, no matter what the consequence.

Meanwhile, Jainab had been inside the house.

'Did you see Sanjida anywhere?' Rasha asked her.

'No. They've locked her in a room.'

Rasha sighed without responding.

'Have you decided what to do?' Jainab asked.

'Not yet.' Rasha shook her head.

'We could try talking to the groom directly. Tell him that the girl is just fourteen. That it's illegal to marry a fourteen-year-old girl. Put some fear into him.'

'Fear of what?'

'Tell him we'll inform the police if he goes ahead with the marriage. That we know the Superintendent of Police and the District Commissioner. Don't you remember, when you showed Razzak Sir's video on the computer, they . . .'

Rasha's eyes began to sparkle. 'I have an idea,' she whispered.

'What idea?'

'I need a mobile phone.'

The light went out of Jainab's face suddenly. 'How will I get hold of a mobile phone now?'

'Needn't be a real one. A toy phone will do!'

'How will I get that either?'

'Something resembling a mobile will do too.'

'Why? What do you plan to do with it?'

'I'll pretend to be talking on the mobile. You see that haggard groom there? I'll speak loudly so that he can overhear me.'

'And what is it that you want him to overhear?'

'I'll pretend to be telling the police that a girl under eighteen is being forced to get married here—and that they should come at once! Something like that.'

Pondering over this for a bit, Jainab nodded. 'Not a bad idea! Might work. That stick of a groom needs a scare. But . . .'

'But what?'

'How will you make sure he hears you?'

'He's sitting by the window, right? I'll talk loudly just outside it, so that he can hear me.'

'But where will you stand? It's full of bushes there . . .'

'Bushes are the best!'

'It won't work if he can't hear you—you'll *have* to make sure somehow that he does.'

'Yes. Let me find out the skeleton's name first. I'll say it out loud several times! He'll get curious and want to find out who it is.'

'You're right.' Jainab nodded.

'Now, what we need is a mobile, or something that looks like one.'

Rasha and Jainab began to look for something suitable. Just then, someone tossed an empty matchbox away after taking the last stick out to light his cigarette. When he had left, Jainab picked up the matchbox. 'Here's your mobile phone!'

'A matchbox?'

'Yes. Hold it so that only the upper half is visible—no one will know what's at the bottom.'

Moving a few steps away, Rasha practised holding the matchbox like a mobile phone. Anyone who didn't know what it really was, would assume she was indeed using a mobile.

Turning to Jainab, Rasha told her, 'Go find out the groom's name.'

Jainab came back a few minutes later. 'The skeleton's name is Rajab Ali. His father's name is—'

'Don't tell me any more, I'll get confused. *Rajab Ali.* Should have been named Rotten Ali! OK, I'm going now,' Rasha told Jainab. 'Say those holy words again.'

Jainab repeated the lines, blowing on Rasha's breast.

Rasha walked through the bushes behind the room all the way to the window. As she was trying to determine whether she was at the right spot, Rajab Ali cleared his throat and spat through the window. It was close, for the gob of spittle missed her head narrowly.

Brandishing the matchbox like a mobile, Rasha said loudly, 'Yes, Rajab Ali . . . Rajab Ali! I just told you his name is Rajab Ali.'

She didn't look at the window directly but it appeared to be working. Rajab Ali was indeed peeping through it upon hearing his name. Pretending not to have noticed, Rasha said, 'Yes, I'm a hundred per cent certain that Sanjida is under eighteen! She goes to school with me, so I know.'

Pretending to listen for a few moments, Rasha continued, 'Look, I'm calling you in secret; we really don't have much time. Can you please put SP Sahib on the line? He had visited our school, and something had happened there after which he and DC Sahib came to know me very well. Tell him Rasha wants to talk to him. *Ra-sha*.'

Waiting for as long as it should take to transfer the call to the SP, Rasha now pretended to be talking to the senior officer.

'Salamalaikum.' A pause. Then, smiling, 'Yes, I'm very well. All of us are very well.' Another pause and then in a serious tone, 'Do you remember seeing a lovely girl with me named Sanjida when you visited our school? Her parents are forcing her to get married! Don't we have a law that makes it illegal to force a girl to marry before eighteen years of age? What about that?'

Once again Rasha pretended to listen to what was being said, responding with an occasional 'hmm'. Then she said excitedly, 'That would be excellent! Excellent. You'll arrest everyone? Handcuffs and ropes? What fun! When will the police come?'

More pretence of listening. Then, 'In half an hour? Good!' A pause. 'No, *of course* I won't tell anyone.' Then, as though she had remembered suddenly, 'Sir, can you send a journalist too? They can get a photo of the arrest! The papers will run a story about the groom being arrested while trying to marry an underage girl.' Rasha giggled.

Without looking up at the window, she confirmed with a glance from the corner of her eye that Rajab Ali had indeed been standing there, listening to everything he needed to. It wasn't necessary to say anything more. Still pretending to talk on the phone, she walked away. Despite an impulse to check on Rajab Ali's expression, she took no risks.

Joining her a little later, Jainab was about to speak, waving her arms and looking up at the window, but Rasha stopped her. 'Don't look too happy, Jainab! Behave normally. Lots of people are going to be keeping an eye on me now, and on you too as a result.'

Suppressing her joy, Jainab whispered, 'You can't imagine the fun!'

'Why? What's happened?'

'I think Rotten Ali has peed his pants out of fear! There's a big uproar in there. They're all whispering furiously with one another.'

Rasha smiled covertly. 'There's something else we have to do.'

'What's that?'

'We have to spread a rumor that policemen have been seen up the road.'

'How?'

'Very simple! We just have to ask a couple of people *why* the police are coming here.'

Rolling her eyes, Jainab nudged Rasha. 'What a devil you are! Full of naught ideas!'

'It's *naughty*, not naught.'

Re-entering the courtyard, Rasha and Jainab asked the first person they met, 'Do you know why the police are coming?'

'*The police?* Why should the police be coming?' the person asked in surprise.

'*I* don't know, that's why I'm asking.'

'Where are they?'

'Up the road. That's what he said.'

'Who?'

Rasha pursed her lips. 'Someone. I don't know him.'

The man nodded and left. They went on and asked another, elderly, person, 'Has anything happened here, Chacha?'

'No. Not that I know of.'

'Then why are the police on their way?'

'Are the police coming *here*?'

'I'm not sure . . .' said Rasha, walking ahead.

Within a few minutes, the rumor had spread all over the house. *The police were coming.* Some even said that they had *seen* the policemen. What ensued was a sight to behold. Removing the garland around his neck and stuffing his cap into his pocket, the groom managed to slip his shoes on and raced away. He was followed by all the middle-aged and old men who had accompanied him.

Rasha saw Sanjida's father asking one of them in surprise, 'Where are all of you going?'

The man snarled, 'This is very bad—getting us here for our boy's wedding and then summoning the police!'

Sanjida's father asked in astonishment, 'What do you mean? When did we call the police?'

The man had no time to explain. He put his shoes on and ran.

Stifling their laughter, Rasha and Jainab ran behind Rajab Ali, shouting, 'Dulabhai! Dulabhai!', as though he really was their brother-in-law.

Looking over his shoulder, Rajab Ali jumped out of his skin.

'Why are you leaving?' Rasha asked sweetly. 'Wait! Sit down. *Please.*'

Pointing at her, the groom stammered, 'Y-y-you . . . y-y-you . . .'

'What about me?'

'You th-think I don't understand? I know ev-everything!'

'What do you know?'

Rajab Ali made no attempt to explain. Abandoning the road, he ran through the middle of the field.

Everyone stood in surprise outside the house, unable to grasp what was going on. Sanjida's father looked around in bewilderment. 'What's happened? I don't understand.'

'All of them started running, screaming that the police are on their way,' someone answered.

'But what's their problem if the police do come? Are they thieves?'

None of those present could answer.

Rasha said, 'Actually, Chacha, just as theft is a crime, so is marrying a girl under eighteen years of age. That's why, I think.'

Sanjida's father looked at Rasha in surprise. 'Who are you?' he asked.

'I study with Sanjida.'

'When did you come?'

'We came running from school as soon as we heard of the wedding.'

Sanjida's father asked on a sudden suspicion, 'What's your name?'

'My name is Rasha.'

His eyes turned into saucers again. 'Are you the girl who ensured that one of your teachers lost his job after you exposed him?'

Rasha wasn't sure whether Sanjida's father meant this to be praise or an accusation. Hesitating, she answered, 'Actually I didn't do anything. The SP and DC Sahibs were present, and they became furious—'

Surmising something, Sanjida's father looked at Rasha sharply. 'Did *you* inform the police?'

'No, I didn't.' After some hesitation, she added, 'But . . .'

'But what?'

'The groom's side *thinks* I did. That's what scared them.'

Sanjida's father gaped at Rasha, looking as though he couldn't believe his ears. He had no idea whether to laugh or be angry.

He was about to speak when Rasha said, 'Just as well they ran away, Chacha.'

'What do you mean, *just as well*?'

'Yes, Chacha, because it has saved *you* from danger too. Getting an underage girl married off is asking for trouble.'

Sanjida's father kept looking at Rasha in disbelief. He still couldn't imagine a girl as young as her was offering him advice like an adult.

He was trying to work himself up to a rage when Rasha said, 'Whatever you may say, Chacha, I didn't care for the groom one bit. Sunken cheeks, skinny, just like a TB patient. He can't even talk properly—I think he stammers. Our Sanjida must marry a smart young man! A doctor or an engineer or a pilot. We'll block his way after the wedding—we won't let him leave till he pays a hundred thousand taka!'

'What! *A hundred thousand!*'

'Yes. It'll be small change for Sanjida's husband.'

'*Small change?*'

'Yes, Chacha. Sanjida is *so* beautiful, it doesn't befit her to have such an ugly husband.'

One of the people standing nearby nodded. 'That's true! The groom looked peculiar.'

'Not just the groom,' added someone else. 'His father looked like a polecat!'

'And it isn't just a matter of looking like a polecat, his behavior is strange too. At first he said that they want no dowry, and now he was saying that there would be no wedding without a motorcycle. Nasty piece of work.'

Sanjida's father sighed. 'Whatever Allah does is probably for the best.'

'That's true, Chacha,' Rasha nodded.

Sanjida's father looked at Rasha, who said, 'May I see Sanjida, Chacha?'

'Yes. Go inside.'

'Chacha. One more thing, Chacha.'

'Yes?'

'Please send Sanjida to school from tomorrow onwards. She's such a good student!'

Directing a long glance at Rasha, Sanjida's father said, 'Very well.'

Sanjida was dressed in a red sari. When she saw Rasha, she hugged her and began to sob.

'What are you crying for, you silly girl?' said Rasha. 'Your groom has run away, you have nothing to worry about any more!' Bringing her lips close to Sanjida's ears, she whispered, 'You look *so* lovely! If I'd been a man, I'd have definitely married you!'

Swatting her head with a fat paw, an elderly woman asked, 'And all this food we cooked, what'll we do with it now?'

Turning to her, Rasha said, 'Don't worry, Fupumma! All our classmates are coming. We came here to fast, but we'll eat our fill instead! Hee hee hee . . .'

Gourango Nana

Jitu came in the morning, his face split into a wide grin.

'It's worked,' he told Rasha.

'What's worked?'

'The road is under water.'

'Which road?'

'The road to school! We don't have to go to school today.' Jitu's grin widened.

'Oh no! What do we do now?'

'Nothing! We're staying home.'

'But we *have* to go to school. How can you forget—our computer lab has just been set up. They're going to deliver the computers.'

Jitu hadn't forgotten, but the joy of not having to go to school surpassed everything else. However, instead of trusting Jitu implicitly, Rasha made some enquiries of her own. It was true—the road to school was indeed under water in places. Part of the road was under knee-deep water, which meant you could walk carrying your shoes in your hands. Over the next few days, the water would rise, becoming chest-high and then, neck-high. Rasha was worried.

During discussions, Jainab said, 'What we need is a boat.'

'*A boat?*'

'Yes. There's no option but to take a boat.'

'How will we get a boat?'

'People in the village have boats; they can be hired.'

'Hire a boat every day?'

'What option do we have?'

Moti was standing nearby. 'With a boat of our own, we could row ourselves to school every day.'

'Do you know how to row?' Rasha asked with a frown.

Moti smiled instead of replying. The kind of smile you get when you ask someone, 'Do you know how to eat?'

'Then why don't we get hold of a boat of our own?' said Rasha.

'How?' asked Jainab.

'That's just what I don't know,' said Rasha, scratching her head.

At night, Rasha asked Nani, 'Do you know where to get a boat, Nani?'

'*A boat?* On the river.'

Rasha shook her head. 'No, that's not what I mean. We need a boat to get to school. Where can we get one?'

Nani thought for a bit. 'Your nana used to have a small boat, but that was a long time ago. I don't know where it's gone. It may have sunk in the canal. Must have been smashed into pieces by now, must have drifted away.'

Rasha said, 'Oh, Nani, why did you let the boat drift away?'

Nani smiled. 'It was such a long time ago. Do you really think it would have survived all these years? You have to look after a boat, repair it regularly, tar it.'

'What do we do then, Nani?'

'Ask around the village—someone may have a small boat that they'll let you use.'

The next day, Rasha took Jainab, Jitu and Moti along for a survey. She discovered to her surprise that practically everyone had a small boat. And those who didn't, had a substitute that they called a *donga*. It was made by carving out a part of the trunk of a palm tree, creating a hollow for one person to sit in and row. But no one had a boat to spare for Rasha and her friends. Disappointed, they were on their way back, animatedly discussing how the problem could be solved, when Jitu said, 'We could make a raft from a banana tree!'

'A raft?'

'Yes. We could take the raft to school.'

Moti was a taciturn sort. Instead of commenting on something, he only smiled.

'What is it? What are you laughing at?' Jitu asked angrily.

'At what you said.'

'What did I say that's so funny?'

'If we have to go to school on a banana raft, we'll have to make two of them every day. One to take to school, one to come back on. Every single banana tree in every village nearby will have to be cut.'

'Why does *every* tree have to be cut?' Jitu shouted. '*Why?*'

At that moment someone said, 'What is it you want to cut?'

They turned to find Salam Nana sitting with his back against a tree. He seemed to have been reading when he was distracted by their loud voices. All four of them greeted him respectfully.

Salam Nana said, 'What's going on, what are you thinking of cutting up early in the morning?'

Rasha smiled. 'Our Jitu Mian wants to cut banana trees to make rafts.'

'*Rafts?* Out of banana trees?'

Rasha went up to Salam Nana to sit near him. So did the others. His crutches were lying by his side—Jitu touched them gingerly.

Rasha said, 'We went out in search of a boat. Since we didn't get one, Jitu suggested making a raft with a banana tree.'

'*A boat?* What do you need a boat for?'

'The road is submerged, so we can't go to school. We could take a boat to school if we had one.'

Salam Nana looked at the group of four carefully. Then he nodded, saying, 'So you aren't looking for a boat to play with but to go to school and study?'

'Ji, Nana,' Rasha nodded. The others followed suit.

'Hmm.' Taking his glasses off and wiping them with the corner of his shirt, he said, 'A noble mission like this must be aided, don't you think?'

Rasha's eyes widened. 'Do *you* have a boat, Nana? Do you?'

'I don't. But so what? I'll get hold of one for you.'

'Really? *Really?*' Rasha's face glowed with happiness.

'Really.'

'How?'

'Getting hold of a boat is hardly a problem in Bangladesh. The entire country runs on them. We were perpetually on boats during the war. In those days, we could around up a dozen boats at half an hour's notice! You think I can't get hold of one during peacetime, for children to take to school? What do you take me for?'

Jainab nodded. 'You can, Chacha! Of course you can, if you want to.'

'Will you *buy* the boat?' Jitu wanted to know.

'Buying is easy. I'll do something better.'

'Tell us what you'll do, Nana, please,' entreated Rasha.

Nana took his glasses off once more to wipe them and then said, 'I have a friend named Gourango. He thatches huts. He makes boats too. I haven't been in touch with him in a long time, but I've been thinking of meeting him. Now I have a reason too! I'll ask him to visit me. We'll catch up on old times, and he'll make you a boat.'

Rasha clapped with joy. '*Make us a boat?* In front of us?'

'Yes, in front of you.'

'How many days will it take, Nana?'

'If he starts in the morning, he can finish making a boat by dusk. Of course, he's getting old now. I don't know if he can still do it in a day.'

'All of us will help him,' Jitu said.

'Then it might take a month!'

Everyone giggled at this.

Jainab said, 'You're right—if Jitu lends a hand, we've had it. A day's work *will* take a month.'

'When will you send word to your friend?' asked Rasha.

'Today. At once!'

'And when will he start work?'

'We'll have to buy some wood, nails, sandpaper, tar and other things. It'll take a little time to put everything together. Let's say the day after tomorrow, or the day after that.'

'Where will it be made, Nana?'

'At your nana's house, Rasha. There's a canal in front. We'll make the boat on the bank and then launch it in the canal.'

'What fun!' Rasha clapped again.

'Yes, lots of fun,' smiled Nana.

Bidding him goodbye, the four of them left for home. Rasha stopped after they had taken a few steps, telling the others, 'Go on ahead, I have to find out something from Salam Nana.'

Rasha ran back to him. 'Nana!'

'Yes?'

'Money will be needed to buy the wood and other things for the boat. And your friend must be paid too. I was thinking . . .'

'What were you thinking?'

'My mother gave me some money before she left. I spent a little from it to get admitted in school. The rest is with me. If we need money to buy the wood—'

'We won't. I have enough wood lying around the house. Nails, tar and sandpaper won't cost much. That leaves Gourango's fees.'

'Ji, Nana.'

'I've told you Gourango is a close friend. A dear friend—like *your* dearest friends. You can make all sorts of demands of your friends, but you cannot offer to pay them. That would be embarrassing.'

'Oh.' It was Rasha's turn to be embarrassed. 'I didn't realize that. Did you fight together in the war?'

'Yes. Gourango, your nana and I—all of us fought in the war together. An educated man and a handyman cannot be friends nowadays. It was possible during the war. Schoolmasters and porters, university students and pickpockets—all became friends with one another. Do you understand?'

'I do.'

'Go now. Your friends are waiting.'

Rasha rose to her feet. 'Nana.'

'Yes?'

'I can't ask Nani to tell me about my nana—she behaves strangely if I do. Some day will you tell me what happened?'

Salam Nana gazed steadily at Rasha. Then he said, sighing, 'I will. I will tell you.'

Salam Nana's friend, Gourango Nana, looked exactly the way Rasha had imagined him to be. Thin, frail, with greying hair and a stubble. His face bore signs of age but his eyes were lively, just like a child's. Salam Nana and Gourango Nana sat side by side, chatting and asking each other about their old friends. They sighed over the ones who had died and talked about those who were alive. Nani sent them cups of tea. Then Gourango Nana got down to work.

Rasha watched him, mesmerized. Salam Nana had already cut the wood. Gourango Nana planed them before sawing them to the right size, using a pencil tucked behind his ear to make markings on the wood. Then he nailed the planks together. Even though Rasha watched with close attention, she could not identify which part of the boat was being built.

Nani had arranged for lunch, which all of them ate together. Rasha had expected Gourango Nana to eat his fill after such hard work but, in fact, he barely touched his food. How could someone who ate *so* little, work *so* hard?

After lunch, he resumed work without a moment's rest. Salam Nana and Gourango Nana were such close friends that they chatted all the time but the funny thing was that once he started work, Gourango Nana didn't say a word—as though his lips had been sewn together.

By the afternoon Rasha could discern the shape of the boat—the two sides had been made. Gourango Nana seemed happy with the measurements, for he proceeded to join the ends. It was indeed a boat now, but so narrow! How would all of them fit in it? But Rasha didn't ask any questions. The whole thing seemed to be like painting a picture. When the artist was halfway through, none of what he was doing made any sense. But when the painting was complete, it all became clear.

Rasha was right. After joining the edges, Gourango Nana turned it upside down, prised it apart with a stick of bamboo and then fixed a plank between the sides. At once the shape of a boat became evident.

'How wonderful!' said Rasha, clapping.

Gourango Nana just looked at her and smiled without a word. He busied himself with the planks. Rasha couldn't believe her eyes when she saw that the boat had indeed been completed before dusk. It was a beautiful boat, looking like a sculpture made by an artist.

Salam Nana began to behave as though it was he, and not Gourango Nana, who had made the boat. Thumping his chest, he said, 'Didn't I tell you my friend will build you a boat, didn't I?'

Rasha said, 'You did, Nana. But I didn't believe you! I thought you were exaggerating because he's a friend.'

'I didn't exaggerate at all. My friend can build an entire boat in a day—if you give him a month, he can build you a ship. Isn't that right, Gourango?'

Gourango Nana chuckled. 'Now you'll say I can build a plane in three months!'

'Of course you can. If you learn plane building, you can certainly build one in three months.'

'Just as well that no one's taught me then, or else this boat would never have been built!'

Rasha said, 'Thank you, Gouranga Nana. Many many thanks!'

'Don't thank me yet, shona,' said Gourango Nana. 'The boat may have been built, but the real work is still to be done.'

'What's that?'

'The holes have to be sealed, the boat has to be tarred, the tar has to dry—and only after that can you launch it.'

Running her hand along the smooth sides of the boat, Rasha said, 'The boat is such a lovely colour now. It'll turn black with the tar!'

'The black will be even more beautiful. Like mahogany. Who told you black is bad? Ask your Salam Nana.'

'What should I ask him?'

'Whether he's happier now that his hair has turned grey than when it was black!'

Rasha giggled, and everyone else joined in.

Putting his tools in a bag, Gourango Nana said, 'That's all for today. I'll tar the boat tomorrow at dawn.'

Nani had asked them to stay for dinner too, but Salam Nana refused. Gourango Nana would eat at his house and stay the night. They had a lot more to talk about.

Rasha saw Salam Nana limp off, leaning on his crutches, with Gourango Nana—his bag slung from his shoulder— by his side. Salam Nana said something and the two of them chortled, one poking the other in the ribs—just like two teenagers.

Salam Nana arrived with Gourango Nana early the next morning. Rasha, Jainab, Jitu Mian, Moti and several other children were already there—waiting for the boat to be completed and launched. Gourango Nana straightened the boat, and began to seal the holes and cracks. Yesterday he hadn't said a word while building his boat, but it wasn't that way today. He kept talking as he worked, even pausing his work at times to say something.

So Rasha said, 'Tell us a story about the war, Nana.'

Both of them stopped talking to look at Rasha. Salam Nana said, 'You want a story about the war?'

'Ji, Nana.'

'A thrilling story!' said Jitu, striking his fist into his palm.

'Which one should I tell them, Gourango?' asked Salam Nana, turning to his friend.

'The one about the ambush you and I laid on the River Baghai!'

'Yes, that's not a bad story at all,' Salam Nana agreed. 'Very well then, listen.'

Taking a few moments to compose his thoughts, Salam Nana began, 'It was roughly the middle of the war. When the war had begun, we hadn't the faintest idea of how to fight. You could say that we didn't know the barrel of a rifle from its butt! We had no idea whether grenades were for throwing or for eating! Anyway, after several false starts, we learnt a little about how to fight. We saw that the bullets fired by the Pakistan military killed us but that our bullets also killed them, if they happened to hit them. Why be afraid then? They were larger in size, they had all kinds of weapons, their uniforms were shiny—while we were practically children, with very few weapons, and there was no question of having shoes and shirts. Most of us were in lungis, and walked barefoot. But none of this was a problem—all we had to do was wait for an opportunity, and fire. The land was ours and so were the people—where could the outsiders hide?

'Gradually we grew bolder. We tried to keep track of their movements, ambushing them whenever we could get details. The monsoon was upon us, which was a bit of a problem. We couldn't rush from one spot to another as before, since we had to take a boat now. But then the Pakistan Army had the same problem. Having grown up next to rivers and lakes, we weren't afraid of water. But *those* fellows' hearts quaked when they saw it! They didn't know how to swim, they were in a state where they could have drowned even in knee-deep water.

'Anyway, we were stationed in this area and had completed several major operations. We had blown up two bridges and a jeep full of Pakistani soldiers. It seemed that their military had now decided to teach us a lesson. Close to 200 Punjabi soldiers arrived, dispatched by headquarters. They were on the far side of the river while we were on this side.

'We had *never* allowed their soldiers to attack us frontally in the past. We always ambushed *them*. This time, we opted for a face-to-face battle. We would occupy bunkers on the riverbank—if they wanted to attack us, they would have to cross the river and we would tear them apart while they were in the water! We took our positions on our side of the river. We had people on the other side too, and kept receiving information from them. In the morning, we were told that the Pakistanis had set off with a huge pile of weapons.

'We were waiting for them to arrive—to cross the river—but they were nowhere to be seen. Suddenly, one of our scouts ran up to us to say that the Pakistani soldiers had split into two groups, one lot approaching us along each bank of the river. Some of the swine had crossed the river all right, but upstream from us, where none of us were stationed. They were professionals, they must have read up war manuals which taught them where and how to cross rivers. We didn't know any of this.

'We were thunderstruck by the scout's information! Our commander was Rasha's Nana, Aziz Master, whom we called Aziz Bhai. He would never be rattled by anything. Taking his time to think deeply, he said, "There are just two dozen freedom fighters here, we cannot fight against several hundreds of their soldiers—all of us will be killed. So we aren't even going to try, we're going to get out of this place at once. If we can get away, well and good. If we're unable to escape, a small group will take up position here, by the road, with a light machine-gun. They will keep the Pakistanis at bay till everyone gets away."

'Aziz Bhai stopped. Then he said, "I need two volunteers." "Why?" I asked. Aziz Bhai said, "I want to teach them a lesson." "How?" I asked. Aziz Bhai said, "They've crossed over to our side of the river, haven't they? So they have to go back too. We have to sink their boats when they're crossing back. The two volunteers have to hide among the hyacinth. With weapons."'

Rasha interrupted the story. 'Wouldn't the weapons get spoilt underwater?'

'No. Immersing them for a very long time might rust them. Mud in the barrel is a problem too. But being underwater for just some time wouldn't do any harm. Anyhow, Gourango and I volunteered. We hid in the water with a rifle each, while the rest left.

'Soon we could hear their soldiers on both banks of the river. They feared for their lives. They kept looking around, moving very slowly and firing. They sent a volley of bullets towards the hyacinth clump too, but, luckily, we were untouched.

'So we practically held our breaths, crouching underwater with only our noses in the air. We could tell that we were being attacked by leeches. The insects must have felt it was Eid, for they hadn't tasted fresh blood in a long time. They sucked so much blood that they bloated and fell off our bodies on their own. We kept our ears open for the sound of sustained gunfire, but there was nothing. Which meant that everyone had got away safely. Aziz Bhai had been clever enough to go across a canal, destroy the bamboo bridge with gunshots and sink the boats, so that the Pakistanis could not follow them.

'Late in the afternoon, we heard the Pakistani soldiers returning. They were very happy, because they were under the impression that they had got rid of the Mukti Bahini from the area. From our hiding spot we could hear the swine abusing the freedom fighters—that we were cowards, that we didn't know how to fight, that we were Indian agents.

This infuriated us further and we were determined to teach them a lesson they wouldn't forget. Today, they would learn what kind of cowards we were!

'Earlier, when they had crossed the river to our side, it was with great care—at a spot far from our location. But now they were certain that we had left, and so there was nothing to fear. They decided to cross right where we were. Making a great commotion as they gathered their boats, they began to cross the river. We realized that this was our chance.

'We allowed them to set off in peace, taking no action as long as there were still some soldiers on our side of the river. When the last of them were on the boat, we swam behind the boats, keeping our heads covered with the hyacinth. Gourango and I went in different directions, waiting for the boats to reach the middle of the river. As soon as they did, we began to fire from two sides.

'That was it! The Bengali boatmen jumped into the water upon hearing the gunfire. The boats began to spin at once. They were closely packed with soldiers, who also started jumping into the water. Some of them even tried to fire back. But the boats capsized and, before they knew it, they were floundering in the water. None of them knew how to swim—they began to sink like stones!

'The soldiers on the other side of the river tried to fire at us but we were out of range, immersing ourselves in the water again with the hyacinth covering our heads—how were they to locate us? We swam underwater for some time and when we surfaced, only one of the boats was to be seen.

And that one boat was drifting along, upside down. Two Pakistani soldiers were clinging to it for dear life, screaming at the top of their voices. We could have finished them off too, but, for some reason, we felt pity for them. It's impossible to kill someone when they're screaming to save themselves. We let those two go.'

'How many Pakistani soldiers were killed, Chacha?' asked Jitu.

'I don't know the exact number. There were three boats—so at least twenty or thirty.'

Shaking his head, Gourango Nana said, 'Must have been more. Those were big boats, there were many soldiers on board. Don't you remember?'

Striking his fist into his palm again, Jitu said, 'Serves them right! What a lesson you taught them!'

Salam Nana nodded. 'Yes, it *was* a big lesson for them. But . . .'

When his words trailed off, Rasha asked, 'But what?'

Salam Nana sighed. He said, 'Two days later, many more soldiers came and burnt down all the houses in the nearby villages, killing everyone and striking terror among the people. So Jitu, war is a terrible thing. We fought because we had no choice. But let our countrymen never have to fight another war. Never. Do you understand?'

Jitu nodded, and so did everyone else.

And so by Boat

Putting his hand on the side of the boat, Jitu Mian said, 'The tar has dried.'

Moti said without touching the wood, 'It hasn't. The tar is nowhere near drying. It's not so simple.'

'It's dry enough,' guessed Rasha. 'Let's launch the boat and test it!'

Moti said, 'Water will seep in if the tar hasn't dried.'

'We'll keep a bowl in the boat to bail out the water!' suggested Rasha.

Jainab insisted, 'We'll get wet tar on ourselves and our clothes.'

'A little tar on the body won't do any harm,' said Rasha.

'You can get rid of it with kerosene!' added Jitu.

'Yes, kerosene is all you need,' Rasha agreed.

'So you won't take no for an answer?' asked Jainab.

Rasha grinned. 'No. I'm getting impatient. Let's go!'

So the four of them pushed the boat into the canal. Gourango Nana had built them a pair of oars too. Moti fetched two long poles of bamboo to use as punts. Jitu found a small plastic bucket to bail out the water if need be.

Nani stood on the bank, watching them get into the boat one by one. Moti sat at the back with the oars, using one of them to push the boat off. The boat was about to spin when Moti stopped it with the oar and then began to row them forward.

Rasha waved her arms with joy, shouting, 'Fantastic!'

As soon as she stood up in her excitement, the boat began to rock! She sat down at once.

'Standing up in the middle of the boat is dangerous,' warned Moti.

'So I see,' said Rasha.

She watched with great interest as Moti rowed. It didn't seem particularly difficult—she was sure she could do it too. Dip the oars into the water and draw them backwards—what could be so hard about that?

'Will you pass me the oar, Moti? I want to try.'

'Have you ever rowed a boat?'

'Never. So what—it doesn't look difficult at all!'

'Does anything look difficult when it's being done? Does cycling look difficult? But have you *any* idea how often you fall when you try to ride a cycle at first?'

'That's true.'

'The canal's narrow here. If you don't row properly, the boat might scrape the banks. There's a lake a little further ahead, plenty of water. You can try there.'

'But when I see you rowing, I want to try at once!'

Moti laughed, showing his pearly white teeth. 'Use the other oar then; we'll get there quicker.'

Rasha picked up the other oar to begin rowing. The boat was about to spin, but Moti kept it going straight. With both of them rowing, they began to move faster.

Jainab said, 'Do you see what's happening because we took the boat out before the tar dried?'

'What's happening?' asked Rasha.

'There's water in the boat!'

Water had indeed collected at the bottom.

'What are you waiting for?' said Rasha. 'Start bailing!'

Jainab and Jitu got down to it.

Soon the canal flowed into a lake. In the dry season, the canal ran through rice fields. But now, with water everywhere, it was difficult to separate the canal from the fields. Trees emerged from the water in places and the tops of bushes were visible sometimes, which made it evident that the water wasn't very deep. It was crystal clear, and the submerged fields could actually be seen under it.

'Let me row by myself now, Moti,' insisted Rasha.

'All right,' said Moti. 'I'll move away, you can sit here.'

Moti shifted and Rasha took his place. The boat rocked dangerously but they managed to steady it.

Rasha began to row on her own and—how strange—the boat continued to move forward!

Having rowed quite a distance, Rasha glanced at the others. 'Did you see that?'

Jainab and Jitu were laughing their heads off for some reason. Moti looked as though he wanted to laugh too, but had stopped himself out of politeness.

'What is it—what are you laughing at?' Rasha asked in surprise.

'At your rowing!' Jitu said.

'Which part of my rowing is making you laugh?'

'Do you know that you've just been going round in circles?'

'Me? Going round in circles?'

'Yes!'

Rasha looked around, and discovered that the boat was indeed moving in a circle and not forward.

'How odd,' she said. 'The boat moves in a straight line when *you* row, Moti. But in circles when *I* do. What's going on?'

Moti smiled. 'That's what you have to learn. That's what rowing a boat is about—you must know how to use the oars so the boat goes straight when you want it to, left when you want it to, right when you want it to.'

'It looks so simple,' said Rasha, 'but it's quite difficult!'

Grimly, Rasha proceeded to learn how to row, her face giving the impression that it was a matter of life and death.

At dinner that night, Rasha asked Nani, 'Have you ever rowed a boat, Nani?'

'What on earth would I do that for?' said Nani in consternation. 'Next thing I know, you'll ask Nani, "Have you ever driven a rickshaw-van?"'

'No, I won't!' said Rasha, laughing.

'Just as well.'

'You see, Nani, you might think it's very easy to row. But it's not that simple actually. If you don't know how to row properly, the boat will keep going round in circles!'

'I don't understand what you're up to. It's all very well to go to school in a boat, but why must *you* be the one to row?'

'Why would I be the only one to row the boat? Everyone will!'

'God alone knows when one of your escapades will get you into trouble.'

Rasha threw a long glance at her grandmother from the corner of her eye and then said, 'Nani.'

'Now what?'

'Do you get upset with me for all these strange things I do?'

Nani smiled. 'Of course not, you silly girl.' After a pause, she said, 'You know what?'

'What, Nani?'

'Now that you're living with me—always up to mischief, asking me a hundred questions—my time passes easily. Earlier, time was a burden—every single thought made me feel like I was going mad. Not any more. I sleep peacefully every night.'

Forgetting that she had morsels of food on her fingers, Rasha hugged her grandmother. 'Really, Nani? You sleep peacefully these days?'

'Yes. I dreamt of your nana last night. Whenever I used to dream of him earlier, it was always of him screaming at being tortured or shot at. I would leap out of bed and stay awake the rest of the night. I couldn't sleep out of fear.'

Rasha listened without interrupting.

Nani went on, 'For the first time last night, I dreamt of your nana in spotless white clothes, a smile on his face. He said, "Well, Zobeda? Have you forgotten me now that your granddaughter is here?" I said, "What are you saying! How can I forget you? Are you well?" He said, "Yes, I am. May I have a glass of water?" I poured him a glass of water from the pitcher. He kept sipping and smiling at me. When I woke up, there was a lovely fragrance of flowers in the room. My heart was full, Rasha.' Nani smiled at her, even though two teardrops trickled down her face.

A letter arrived for Rasha from Australia the next day. Since it was from a foreign country, the postman had to be given a tip. Rasha was afraid of what she'd find in it, but still she had to open it.

There was a card inside, a photograph of kangaroos on a field. Along with it, a letter from her mother with descriptions of Australia—how beautiful the shops were, how many exciting things they sold, how clean the streets were, how courteous everyone was and so on. It was summer in Bangladesh but winter in Australia—that was mentioned too. There was nothing more, neither about herself nor about Rasha. It wasn't a letter from a mother to her daughter, it was a letter to the editor of a newspaper.

The letter embarrassed Rasha more than it saddened her. But she wasn't sure whom she was embarrassed for.

Everyone was quite keen to take the boat to school. No one sat still in it—they either rowed or used the punting pole. So the small boat raced along like a canoe! Not just that, once they got to the river, they even cut across the curves sometimes. There was knee-high water and even mud sometimes, so they had to get out, push the boat through these sections, and then rejoin the river. Their arms and legs and entire bodies were covered in water and mud by the time they got to school. Even their books were sopping wet, but none of them cared very much. They were enjoying their days. The computer laboratory had been set up in school; desks and chairs had been fitted. The computers would arrive any day now. Rasha had made enquiries—letters were being exchanged.

The monsoon had arrived. At first, there were sporadic showers. Now it rained regularly. And what torrential rain—Rasha stared at it in wonder. She didn't know if there was any sound on earth sweeter than of raindrops drumming on a tin roof. The trees were a dense green, the leaves fat and lively. It seemed that the greenery would burst from the earth everywhere! The trees weren't trees, they were living creatures. The canal in front of the house was filled with water, the strong current making it flow noisily. What used to be fields was all covered with water now—Nani's house was like an island in the middle of the ocean.

There was mud wherever the ground was not submerged, slushy and sticky. Try as she might, Rasha just could not get used to it. Eventually, she had to give up and take shelter inside the house. She sat by the window, studying, while the downpour continued relentlessly. She had leafed through the books that Jahanara Madam had sent earlier—now she began to read them in earnest. They seemed a little difficult at first, but, once she began to concentrate, she derived an unusual pleasure from them. She had no idea that mathematics could be so interesting. What excited her the most was physics—she was astonished by the things Einstein had accomplished with the special theory of relativity. She couldn't believe what she was reading! Rasha devoured her science books the way people read detective novels.

Nani observed her and shook her head ruefully. 'I don't understand your ways. How can someone be bent over their books day and night? It's not even as though you have exams or something.'

'Come sit with me, Nani,' Rasha said. 'I'll explain special relativity to you—you'll be stunned!'

'For heaven's sake,' said Nani. 'I've barely managed to get my head in order; you want to turn it upside down again?'

Something funny happened one day. After a long period, when she'd had her nose buried in her books, Rasha discovered that she had run out of notebooks. Going to the market was not an easy matter. She gave Moti some money, asking him to request anyone going to the market to get some notebooks for her.

Two days later, Moti brought her four notebooks, neatly tied up in newspaper sheets. Unwrapping the notebooks, Rasha was about to throw the newspaper sheets away when she stopped suddenly upon discovering an all too familiar illustration. A very old man stood there while a rocket was flying overhead, with a much younger man in it. The story of these two brothers was always used to describe the theory of relativity—one twin returns from a voyage on a rocket to discover that the other one has aged significantly. Rasha read the article with great interest. Someone had written about the theory of relativity in the 'Science' section of the newspaper—written quite well, in fact. The writer knew how to simplify complex ideas.

Turning the page over, Rasha found the words 'Science Olympiad' printed in large type on one corner, followed by ten science questions. Those who could answer the ten questions correctly would be invited to a national Olympiad in Dhaka. But the headmaster of the school would have to certify that the student had indeed written the answer by himself or herself, without anyone's help. Answers had to be sent within a week. The newspaper was three days old, which meant that there were just four days to go.

Rasha sat on her bed with the newspaper. The first three questions were ridiculously simple. She knew how to work out the answers to the next three, but she would need pen and paper. The answers to the remaining four eluded her—she would have to think about them. Rasha pondered, biting her pencil.

At dinner, Nani asked, 'What are you thinking so hard about, Rasha?'

'A man goes into space in a rocket. On the way back—'

'Must you think about this during dinner?'

Rasha smiled helplessly at Nani. 'It's stuck in my head, I can't get rid of it!'

'Get it out. Else you'll be in my state. Everything upside down!'

Rasha giggled, but she *couldn't* get it out of her head. She thought about it through the meal, she thought about it when helping her grandmother with the dishes, she thought about it when brushing her teeth, she thought about it when she went to bed. And just as she was about to fall asleep, she sat bolt upright. The solution had come to her like a flash of lightning! She felt the urge to light a lamp at once and work the problem out on paper, but she decided not to. Nani was curled up on the floor—she would wake up if Rasha lit the lamp. Her grandmother used to toss and turn all night long earlier but now that she slept peacefully, Rasha didn't have the heart to disturb her.

The next day, Rasha worked out the answers to two more problems. That left her with just one, but she simply couldn't crack it. She hit a wall every time she tried. It seemed to her that she needed a different sort of mathematics to solve *this* particular problem. Eventually she gave up, and decided to send the answers that she had actually been able to work out. She would have to courier them from the market and get the headmaster's signature before that. There was no time at all!

It had been drizzling since morning and the school was shut. She would have to meet the headmaster at his residence. If she left at once, she would be able to finish all she had to do and be back home by evening. So Rasha didn't delay.

Jainab was visiting her fupu, there was no sign of Moti, and Jitu was shivering with fever under a quilt. Rasha knew several of the other children in the village but she couldn't find any of them, which meant that she would have to go alone. This wasn't entirely unusual—sometimes she had rowed herself to school alone.

So Rasha packed her things in a polythene packet and set off. Rowing along the canal, she reached the lake and then cut across through the middle to enter the narrow river. Not that it was narrow any more, having swollen with rainwater. Rasha guided her small boat close to the bank, crossing over to the other side near the bridge. Mooring the boat near the market, she stepped on land. A boatman, whom she and her friends knew, was always stationed here, which meant that there was no fear of their boat being stolen.

Rasha was sopping wet but she no longer cared about these things. She used to be under the impression that getting drenched in the rain meant getting a fever, but here she had realized that this was nonsense. One could stay out in the rain as long as one wanted—it did no harm. Most people in this land worked in the rain, but no one fell ill or got a fever as a result.

Rasha went to the headmaster's house, which she knew but had never visited. She was worried he might not be home—which would create huge problems—but it turned out that he was there.

An astonished headmaster asked, 'What's all this? Where have you turned up from, all wet in the rain? What's the matter?'

Rasha explained everything to the headmaster, but he didn't appear to get it. Staring at her for some time, he said, 'You've done all these sums and then come to me in the rain so that I can sign them?'

'Ji, sir.'

'How will that help?'

'The people I have to send them to will be assured that it's I who's solved the problems, that no one else did them for me.'

'And then?'

'Those who get the answers right will be invited to an Olympiad. A Science Olympiad!'

'What's that?'

Rasha scratched her head. 'I'm not sure, sir.'

'You're not sure?'

'No, sir.'

'You've done all this without being sure?'

'I think it's an exam or something.'

'A talent exam?' asked the headmaster, frowning.

'Maybe, sir. It might be something like that.'

The headmaster signed the papers. He had a school seal at home, which he stamped on them. Rasha went to a courier, requesting that the papers be delivered the next day to the address that she had copied from the newspaper.

When she was done, Rasha went to a shop to buy a small bottle of coconut oil for her grandmother. For herself, she bought a few more notebooks and two ballpoint pens. Her grandmother massaged her head with coconut oil with or without reason—she believed that it kept the mind calm. So Rasha would buy coconut oil for her whenever she could.

She went back to her boat with the notebooks, pen and coconut oil, and set off for home. Once past the bridge, she rowed close to the bank. The drizzle had intensified, the raindrops making strange sounds on the river water. Rasha rowed swiftly. The bank was dotted with small, inhabited villages. But once she entered the lake, there wouldn't be a soul on either bank. She would have to cross it diagonally. Whenever Jitu was with her, he would spin eerie, ghostly yarns about the lake. Although Rasha didn't believe any of them, she was suddenly reminded of them now. The rain was lashing down when she entered the lake. Water was all she could see in every direction. Visibility was very low. She knew the direction now but when she could no longer see the banks, how would she know which way to go? What if she got lost? What if it got dark? What if she could never get out? Rasha's heart jumped into her mouth.

Rasha tried her best to keep the boat pointing in the right direction, without meandering. She would be marooned in this desolate area if that happened. She could have got her bearings from the villages visible in the distance had it not been raining.

Suddenly she heard a tinkling sound, like a dancer in anklets. Rasha was startled, and that was when she saw something floating towards her. It had four red flags on its four corners, while the surface was covered with a sheet. Rasha peered at it curiously in the rain, realizing that it was a raft. Beautifully decorated, but empty. There must have been a bell fixed on it somewhere, pealing in the wind.

Rasha guided her boat closer to the raft and surveyed it. At once she screamed in terror. A girl lay on the raft, dead. Rasha had never seen a corpse before, but she had no difficulty understanding that this was a dead body. The girl had been dressed in a lovely sari but it had been swept away in the water. Her eyes were slightly open, and her teeth could be seen though parted lips. She looked as though she would sit upright any moment.

Pushing the raft away, Rasha began to row with all her might, but she noticed in horror that the raft was following her. She began to tremble with fear, convinced that the corpse would stand up any minute and laugh menacingly. Or that it would grab her boat and climb aboard. Rasha knew that a corpse could never do any of this, but still she trembled uncontrollably with an indescribable fear as she kept rowing with all her strength.

She was afraid to look behind her, but she could hear the tinkling sound fading into silence. Then she looked back apprehensively, spotting the raft drifting in the distance. So eerie! So chilling!

That night, Rasha went to sleep holding her grandmother.

Nani read the Ayatul Kursi for her, saying, 'I get worried about you sometimes.'

Rasha nodded. 'You're right, Nani. I get worried about myself too sometimes.'

'Why did you have to cross the lake alone?'

'I didn't *want* to go alone, but since I couldn't find anyone to come with me . . .'

'Don't go there again.'

'All right, Nani. I won't.'

'So many dangers everywhere . . .'

'What can a corpse do, Nani?'

'I don't fear dead people. I fear living ones. Have you any idea how many scoundrels there are in the world?'

'I have an idea.'

'So you must be careful.'

'I will, Nani.'

After a pause, Rasha sighed. 'Nani.'

'Now what?'

'Why did they cast her off on a raft?'

'She must have been bitten by a snake. This is what they do with people who die of snakebite.'

'Why, Nani?'

'People believe that the dead person drifts along to the house of a snake exorcist, who can bring them to life again.'

'How is that possible? Can a dead person come to life?'

'It *shouldn't* be possible,' Nani said with a sigh. 'But those who love you want to believe it is. No one can accept death. No one.'

Nani fell silent abruptly, her eyes empty.

Rasha woke up with a start in the middle of the night. She felt as though the girl in the raft was tugging at her arm, saying, '*Why did you leave me? Come with me. Come.*'

Rasha lay in silence with her arms around her grandmother.

Makku Chora's Wife

Everyone was bathing in the lake in the afternoon. Rasha told Jainab, 'Let's see who can stay underwater longer!'

'All right,' said Jainab.

'Me too,' said Jitu.

'It's no use competing with you,' teased Rasha. 'You're not human, you're a fish!'

'Stranger! You're stranger!' Jitu giggled.

Then the three of them dived in together.

Rasha was no longer afraid of the water. She could swim now, even if not as well as Jitu. She could go from one end of the lake to the other, all the while underwater. They had recently started this new game, competing to see who could stay under the surface the longest. At first, Rasha could barely survive a few seconds before gasping. But now she could spend long stretches underwater. Today, too, she beat Jainab. There was no question of defeating Jitu, of course—no one knew how he managed to stay under as long as he did. He would surface with a whoosh after a long time.

'How do you manage to stay under for so long, Jitu?' asked Rasha.

'Are you planning to be Makku Chora when you grow up?' added Jainab.

'*Makku Chora?*' asked Rasha. 'That fellow we met? The one with the pretty wife?'

'Yes. He can stay submerged for hours!'

'Nonsense!' said Rasha. 'No one can stay underwater for hours. We can't live more than a few minutes without breathing! We need oxygen.'

'Makku Chora doesn't need oxygen,' said Jitu. 'He breathes underwater, like fish.'

'Rubbish!'

'I swear by the Lord. Makku Chora has gills!'

Rasha's eyes widened. 'Have you *seen* his gills? Where are they?'

'I haven't actually seen them, but I've seen him stay underwater for two hours.'

'Don't lie,' said Rasha. 'A man who can stay underwater for two hours without breathing can make millions by showing his trick to the world! He won't have to earn a living by theft.'

Jitu said, 'Makku is addicted to stealing. He can't live without it.'

'Say that. But don't say that he can stay submerged for two hours without breathing!'

'He does!' Jitu looked obstinate. '*Two hours.*'

'Don't lie,' repeated Rasha. 'I'll smack you!'

Jainab said, 'He isn't lying, Rasha. Makku Chora can actually do it.'

'Impossible.'

'Everyone's seen it. He was running away after stealing something and then he jumped into the water. And he just wouldn't get out. They had to use a fishing net!'

'Impossible!'

'It's true,' said Jainab. 'Ask the others if you don't believe me.'

When Rasha asked other people, all of them—amazingly—said that it was true. These kind of stories are usually second-hand information, but this time Rasha actually found people who had seen it for themselves. Makku Chora had indeed remained underwater for two hours—they'd had to cast a net to pull him out.

Rasha decided to ask Makku herself. She set off for his house one afternoon with Jitu in tow. Ever since her first visit to his home, she had remembered his pretty wife more clearly than Makku himself.

The last time Makku had been making something with strips of bamboo. Today he was winding strands of rope around his foot. He threw a suspicious look at Rasha and Jitu.

'How are you, Makku Chacha?' asked Jitu.

Makku emitted an indistinct sound through his nose.

Jitu said, 'Rasha Apu is here to see you.'

Makku looked at her with slitted eyes without saying a word.

Jitu said, 'There's something we want to know from you.'

Makku spoke for the first time. 'Know what?'

Rasha took a step forward and said, 'Apparently you can stay underwater without breathing.'

Makku continued to peer at her suspiciously.

'Can you?' Rasha continued.

This time, Makku nodded tentatively.

'Really?'

Makku nodded again.

Rasha said, 'But what you're saying is impossible! No one can survive beyond a minute or two without breathing. You need oxygen to stay alive. Without oxygen, the brain is damaged.'

Makku Chora continued winding the strands wordlessly. It made no difference to him whether the lack of oxygen damaged the brain or not.

Rasha asked, 'Will you tell us how you stay submerged?'

Makku continued with what he was doing, pretending not to hear her.

'*Will you tell us?*' Rasha repeated.

Makku was silent this time too.

Rasha tried once more. '*Please!* Will you?'

Makku spat through his teeth. 'My ustad's blessings,' he said.

'*Blessings?*' Rasha looked at him in surprise. 'Ustad's blessings?'

Now Makku's pretty wife emerged from the room to stand with her hand on the door.

'How are you?' asked Rasha, turning to her.

She nodded without a word to say that she was well.

Rasha turned back to the thief. 'You're saying that it's your ustad's blessings. But with or without his blessings, you still have to breathe! How will a man survive otherwise?'

Makku continued to wind the strands of rope with great attention, seeming to all the world that he didn't even know that Rasha was there.

Giving up, Rasha said, 'Very well—if you won't tell us, what can we do. But if you really can stay underwater without breathing for an hour or two, you can earn millions by demonstrating this feat to people.'

Makku showed no interest in earning millions. He wound the strands of his rope with undivided concentration.

'Let's go, Jitu,' said Rasha.

'Let's,' said Jitu.

'We're leaving, all right?' Rasha told the pretty wife.

She half-nodded.

Rasha and Jitu were some distance from Makku's house already when they heard a voice behind them.

'You, girl!'

Rasha turned back to see Makku's pretty wife walking towards them. Rasha went up to her in surprise, who said, 'You came to find out how he can stay underwater?'

'Yes. No one can stay submerged for an hour or two without breathing.'

'He breathes.'

'*How* does he breathe?'

'He has a pipe. Either a bamboo pipe, or the stalk of a papaya leaf. At the very least, a stalk of jute. He uses it to breathe even when he's underwater.'

Rasha's eyes brightened. 'So clever!' she said in surprise. 'So simple. And there he was, telling me it's his ustad's blessings!'

Makku's wife's face hardened. In a low voice, she said, 'His ustad's blessings are no blessings.'

She was about to return when Rasha called her back. 'Just a minute.' She stopped.

Rasha said, 'I've never seen anyone as beautiful as you. Do you know how pretty you are?'

Makku's wife was silent for a while. Then she said, 'Can I tell you something, girl?'

'Of course.'

'Women from poor families have no greater curse than beauty. I always plead to God—*whatever you might want to do, don't make the women of poor families beautiful.*'

She walked away without another word.

Rasha suddenly felt sad, though she didn't know why. She stood there for a long time.

Finally Jitu said, 'Let's go, Rashapu.'

Sighing, Rasha said absently, 'Yes, let's go.'

The idea of using a pipe to breathe underwater *seemed* very simple, but Rasha discovered that doing it was anything but easy. The first time she tried, she inhaled water and made a mess of it. Jitu claimed that the water had passed through her nostrils and entered her brain. He even had some cataclysmic stories about the damage that water could cause if it got into the brain, but Rasha paid no attention. The others gave up after one or two attempts, but Rasha did not. She discovered that she *could* use the pipe to breathe if she pinched her nostrils shut with her fingertips. People didn't usually hear themselves breathe but when one breathed through a pipe underwater, one could hear the sound clearly—it was like an engine running.

It took Rasha a couple of weeks to become an expert at breathing underwater. She used the stalk at the base of a papaya leaf. Rasha had decided to buy a long rubber pipe the next time she went to the market, and use it to practise underwater breathing while submerged in the lake. What fun it would be!

Rasha had no idea how amazing the underwater world was. But it wasn't easily visible, because everything was indistinct under the surface. Divers put on goggles, which ensures that there is no water directly in front of their eyes, enabling them to see clearly. Goggles like these were obviously not going to be available in the village market. So Rasha was working out how to make a pair for herself. It was impossible to think of this marvellous underwater world remaining invisible—she simply *had* to get a view!

It had been a long while since Rasha had sent off the answers for the Science Olympiad. She had been very excited for the first few days after that, expecting a reply soon. But there had been none. Maybe the couriers hadn't been able to deliver her answers in time, or maybe they hadn't arrived at all. Or—who knew—maybe they had indeed reached the people at the Olympiad, but her answers had turned out to be wrong. Or perhaps some of her answers were right, but the others may have done even better.

After a week or two of enthusiasm, Rasha forgot about it—one reason for which was the arrival of the computers at school. Razzak Sir had been given the responsibility of the laboratory earlier, but he had lost his job. Gouri Madam was in charge now. She had been away for a long time to receive training but it wasn't clear how well it had gone, because she was looking sort of nervous.

The headmaster and other teachers had been bustling about when the computers were being installed. Afterwards, only Gouri Madam remained in the computer laboratory, standing nervously in the middle. She was holding some papers, which she consulted, and then glanced anxiously at the computers, unable to understand where she should start.

Rasha waited till there was no one nearby before peeping into the laboratory to ask, 'May I come in, madam?'

'Who is it?' asked Gouri Madam. 'Oh, Rasha? Come on in.'

Looking at the rows of computers, Rasha said, 'So beautiful, aren't they, madam?'

'They are. All because of you!'

'Not just me, madam. Everyone else too.'

Scratching her head, Gouri Madam said, 'All these computers—shouldn't they have also given us someone to look after them? How can I look after so many computers all by myself?'

'Something will be worked out, madam.'

'I hope so.' Gouri Madam snorted.

'When will our computer classes start?' asked Rasha.

'Soon. In a few days.'

'Madam?'

'What is it?'

'May I switch one of them on and see what software they've installed?'

'*Switch one on?* Be careful—don't spoil it.'

'No, madam, I won't.'

Rasha sat down in a corner and switched on one of the computers. It was a brand new machine, still smelling of fresh plastic. The operating system had only just been installed—it came up on the monitor in a few moments. Rasha smacked her lips, as though savouring something delicious.

After exploring the computer for some time, Rasha said joyfully, 'Madam!'

'What?'

'It's connected to the Internet, madam. Mind-blowing speed!'

'Really?'

'Ji, madam. See.' Her fingers raced over the keyboard, calling up a picture of Einstein on the screen.

'Where did you get this?'

'Google.'

Gouri Madam didn't appear to understand.

Rasha checked her email after a long time. So much mail! But most of it useless. She sighed as she scanned them.

Staring at Rasha enviously, the teacher asked, 'You know how to use a computer?'

'I can, madam. It's my best friend!'

Gouri Madam lowered herself gingerly on a chair and fiddled with the mouse. It was obvious that she wasn't used to it at all.

'The book says it'll open if you click twice, but it's not opening,' she muttered to herself. 'What's the problem?'

Rasha wasn't sure whether to speak but she ended up telling the teacher, 'You have to double-click quickly, madam.'

'I thought I *was* doing it quickly. This computer seems a little too fast!' Gouri Madam laughed nervously at her own joke.

A little later, she muttered again, 'They told me you can type in Bangla. But see, you only get English letters if you press these keys. What a nuisance!'

Rasha hesitated again before answering. 'The font hasn't been selected yet. It'll appear in Bangla if a Bangla font is selected.'

'Of course, of course,' said Gouri Madam, caught off guard.

At first, she was embarrassed to ask Rasha for help, but she overcame her hesitation quite quickly, and kept asking questions every time she had problems. Some of the questions were so silly that Rasha was tempted to laugh, but she explained everything gravely.

With Rasha by her side, Gouri Madam finally gained some courage. They switched on all the computers.

Trying out each of them, Rasha said, 'All OK, madam.'

'Good!'

'Then shall we have classes from tomorrow?'

'*Tomorrow?*' Madam looked worried. 'Don't we need to make a timetable first?'

'Can't we do that later, madam? Let everyone try these out first.'

'Are you crazy?' Gouri Madam said in consternation. 'If they make mistakes, the whole thing will blow up!'

'They won't, madam. I'll be here if you like. I won't let anyone make any mistakes.'

'You'll be here?'

'If you want me to.'

'All right, let's try then!'

And so Rasha began to be seen in the computer laboratory all the time. Computers would have been a very difficult subject—impossible to grasp—had Gouri Madam been the teacher. But because Rasha did the demonstrations, everyone realized that the computer was actually a toy. A toy that none of them had expected to have so much fun with!

Gouri Madam discovered helplessly that it had taken the children only a few days to know more about computers than she did. What was more—while her own knowledge was sketchy at best, they had figured it out thoroughly! The students began to use the computers in ways that flabbergasted her.

One day, the headmaster sent for Rasha. She went to his room anxiously, wondering if she had overstepped her limits with the computers, or whether someone had complained about her.

Poking her head in, she asked, 'May I come in, sir?'

'Come.'

Rasha went up to the headmaster. Looking at her over his glasses, he held out an envelope towards her.

'There's a letter from Dhaka. From the Science Olympiad committee.'

Rasha's heart lurched. 'What have they said, sir?' she asked.

'They've said that there's going to be a Science Olympiad in Dhaka, for which you've been selected. I don't quite understand—I thought Olympics were for sports! How will there be a Science Olympiad? Are people going to run holding test tubes? Or will they have to jump with microscopes?' The headmaster burst out laughing, as though he had made a brilliant joke.

Rasha said, 'I think there will be science questions to be answered.'

The headmaster scanned the letter once more. Then he said, 'If you go to Dhaka, they'll put you up in a girls' hostel, pay for your travel and give you an allowance. Want to go?'

Controlling her excitement, Rasha confirmed, 'Yes, sir, I want to go.'

Scratching his ear, the headmaster said, 'It's a matter of prestige for the school. You should definitely go! But how? Who will go with you?'

'Won't we find someone?' asked a worried Rasha.

'Let's see if I can convince one of the teachers.'

On her way back from school, Rasha told everyone that she was going to Dhaka to participate in the Science Olympiad. That she would be given travel expense and an allowance. That a minister would distribute the prizes. Everyone marvelled at this news. Jitu was the one most excited, telling everyone in the village once they were back. It wasn't as though what he said was entirely accurate—he exaggerated recklessly whenever he felt the need.

Possibly because of Jitu's efforts in spreading the news, Salam Nana arrived that evening to meet Rasha, calling out from the yard, 'Where are you, Rasha Beti?'

Rasha came out with a lantern to discover it was him. 'Oh, it's you, Nana,' she said, flustered. 'Come in, come in.'

Salam Nana said, 'No, I won't stay. I heard something from Jitu. Apparently a minister is going to give you a prize! What's going on?'

Rasha said in embarrassment, 'No, I'm not getting a prize or anything. That naughty Jitu says anything he likes!'

Salam Nana smiled. 'Our Jitu is Reuters,' he said. 'He always passes the news on!'

'It's not news at all—all he spreads are rumours. He can lie so much!'

'Never mind,' said Salam Nana. 'Maybe he exaggerated a bit. Why don't you tell me the real story? Something must have happened—what is it?'

'There's going to be a Science Olympiad in Dhaka. I've been selected to take part.'

'*A Science Olympiad?* What's that?'

'Even I don't know very well,' said Rasha. 'I think it's some sort of science examination.'

'How did they select you?'

'They had advertised the event with ten questions, which I sent the answers to.'

'Splendid!' Salam Nana nodded in delight. 'How wonderful! You're a worthy granddaughter of our Aziz Master. Now let's see what prize you can bring back.'

Rasha said, 'There'll be hundreds of boys and girls there. Why would *I* win a prize?'

'I'm sure you will! Not that it matters if you don't. Participating is the main thing.' Salam Nana began to limp off on his crutches.

'Won't you come in, Nana?' asked Rasha.

'No, Rasha. I'll go now.'

Rasha said, 'Let me walk with you part of the way.'

'Come along then. See how beautiful the moonlight is! I don't think there's anything as beautiful on earth as the moonlight.'

Rasha walked along the canal with Salam Nana. 'Nana,' she said.

'Yes?'

'Do you know how my grandfather died?'

Salam Nana sighed. 'As a matter of fact, no one knows. We came hereabouts on an operation. It ended just before evening. Your nana said, "Now that I'm so close to home, let me pay my wife and child a visit." I told him not to go. I said, "The razakars are very active in this area, it's best not to go."

'There was a deluge. Your nana said, "No one's going to come out in this rain. I'll just see my daughter once and come back."

'Giving me his gun, he said, "Keep this." I kept it. Now I think it would have been better if he'd taken it—he could have at least finished off some of the traitors. He wouldn't have been caught either. The man was as brave as a lion.

'Anyhow, Aziz Bhai went home, met your grandmother—even saw your mother. As he was about to leave, your nani suggested that he wait till the torrential rain stopped.'

Salam Nana paused, sighed, and said, 'Death must have been stalking Aziz Bhai. Why would he have delayed his return otherwise? Meanwhile, the razakars arrived and surrounded the house.

'No one knows exactly what happened after that. The razakars took him away—we heard that they were going to hand him over to the Pakistan Army. But they didn't. And nothing was heard of him afterwards. They must have killed him that night.'

'Doesn't anyone know where they buried him?' asked Rasha.

'No one knows. In fact . . .'

'In fact, what?'

'Did his captors even bury him? They did not—they must have just killed him and dumped the body somewhere! Those razakars are not human. They're beasts—they're worse than beasts. There won't be room for them even in hell!'

'What happened to the razakars?'

'The freedom fighters killed some of them after the war. Some escaped. Some of them were caught and imprisoned. They were released when the razakars were pardoned in 1975.'

'Is it true, Nana, that our school is named after . . .'

Salam Nana sighed deeply. 'It's true. I believe he was among the ones who captured your nana.'

'A school named after a razakar? How could this be possible?'

'It was wrong. But what can you do? Several of the recent governments have been trying to please the razakars. After his release from jail in '75, Ahad Ali was quiet for a few years. Then he was elected as chairman, made pots of money, set up a madrasah named after himself, set up a school too. He was even on the committee but now that he's become old, he doesn't go out any more.'

'Have you ever seen him, Nana?'

'No, I haven't. Why?'

'I want to find out what a razakar looks like.'

'They look just like human beings. They have noses and mouths and eyes like everyone else. But they aren't really human. They're beasts. Worse than beasts.'

Rasha walked in silence beside Salam Nana. His crutches kept sinking into the moist soil, but still its sound could be heard. The sound of a freedom fighter's suffering.

The Science Olympiad

The college girl stared at Rasha in surprise and then asked, 'What are you doing here?'

'I've come for the Science Olympiad.'

'*The Science Olympiad?*' The girl looked at her friend in astonishment. 'Is there an Olympiad for children too?'

'Not that I know of. It's just one Olympiad.'

'Which class are you in?' the college girl asked Rasha.

'Class eight.'

'How did you get a chance to join the Olympiad in class eight? All the questions are of Intermediate level!'

A bright-looking girl chuckled. 'Don't you get it? All you need is someone at home going to Intermediate university. They'll solve all the problems for you.'

Rasha's ears reddened, but she didn't respond.

The bright-looking girl turned to her. 'That wasn't a good thing to do, Apu!'

Rasha shook her head. 'It's seeming like it wasn't.'

'Getting grown-ups to solve the problems . . .'

'That's not what I'm talking about.'

'Then what are you talking about?'

'I'm talking about being here. It seems to me that I wasn't right to come here—because if all of you somehow get to know that I solved the problems myself, you'll feel very bad for saying all these things without knowing the truth.'

Suddenly the college girls fell silent.

The headmaster had personally escorted Rasha. He had disappeared after taking her to the girls' hostel. He could be present at the Olympiad tomorrow, or not. He would take Rasha back the day after tomorrow, at the end of the prize distribution ceremony. He had told Rasha that he had various things to do in Dhaka, which would take all day. Rasha had not objected. She had a place to sleep at night, her meals were taken care of too. They would take her to the venue in a bus and bring her back—so there was nothing to worry about.

At night she discovered that the lights in the hostel were very bright, hurting her eyes. Living by the light of lamps and lanterns in the village had meant that her eyes could no longer stand the glare of electric lights. How strange!

Rasha got herself ready early the next morning. Most of the participants who had come from outside Dhaka were staying with relatives. So there weren't many girls in the hostel. She had bathed at the crack of dawn, dressed, eaten her breakfast in the canteen and was now waiting downstairs. Her one fear—what if the bus left without her?

The bus arrived exactly at nine. It couldn't leave her behind—she was the first to get on board. It took them to the venue of the Science Olympiad—an enormous field with a gigantic marquee. There was a large stage on one side, with a glittering digital banner behind it. Participants were queuing up to register. Most of them were college students, older than her. There were very few boys and girls of her age. Rasha too stood in the queue and registered, getting a lanyard with her name on a card to wear around her neck, along with the rules of the Olympiad, her daily allowance and travel reimbursement. Participants crowded around a counter which served complimentary noodles.

The inaugural ceremony was still half an hour away. Rasha was wandering around aimlessly when she suddenly spotted Jahanara Madam. She ran up to her, practically shouting, 'Madam! Madam!'

Jahanara Madam turned towards her. It took her a moment to recognize Rasha, her eyes reflecting surprise and then joy.

Taking Rasha in her arms, she said, '*You, Rasha*? At this Olympiad?'

'Ji, madam.'

'Aren't you in class eight? This is a college-level competition!'

'Don't you remember the books you sent me? I read them . . .'

Jahanara Madam's face was suffused with a huge smile. 'You've read them?'

'I haven't finished . . .'

'How will you finish so soon? At your age, even starting on them is difficult!'

'I can't understand everything—every now and then there's a "dy divided by dx" . . .'

'Calculus. That's calculus.'

'I don't know it, so it proves a little difficult.'

'I'll buy you a fantastic book on calculus—you won't have problems any more!' Jahanara Madam patted Rasha on her head. 'I never imagined you would seriously read those books . . .'

'The thing is, you can't imagine how much it rains in the monsoon. There's water everywhere, you can't get out of the house. So I read instead. By lamplight, at night . . .'

'No electricity?'

'Nothing at all.'

'But Rasha, you look very fresh. Sunburnt, but fresh. Spirited!'

Rasha nodded. 'You have to be spirited, madam. We take a boat to school in the monsoon. We row ourselves.'

Jahanara Madam looked at her in surprise. 'You can row a boat?'

'I can do many other things too, madam!'

'What other things?'

'Swim. Climb trees. Cook a little. Get beaten up by teachers. Quarrel . . .'

'What's your school like?' asked Jahanara Madam, laughing.

Rasha lowered her voice. 'Very bad. We're hardly taught anything. The teachers know very little, they can't teach either—we have to study on our own.'

'That's not a bad thing in a way, it builds self-confidence.'

Rasha looked around. 'Isn't anyone from our class here?'

'No. Some students from the collegiate section are here.'

'I don't know them.'

'No, you don't.'

Jahanara Madam practically clung to Rasha. 'Should I ask you about your mother, Rasha?' she said.

Rasha tried to laugh cheerfully. 'It's best if you don't, madam.'

'Very well, I won't then.'

'Ammu sends postcards from Australia sometimes.'

'I see.' Jahanara Madam continued after a pause. 'And your nani?'

'Nani's very well. She's very sweet.'

'Good! Everyone needs one or two sweet people in their lives.'

'My friends are sweet too.' Rasha smiled.

'That's wonderful . . .' Jahanara Madam wanted to continue but there was an announcement asking everyone to take their places, for the inaugural ceremony was about to start. Jahanara Madam took Rasha towards the marquee.

Rasha had expected the ceremony to be a long and annoying one, with a succession of speeches, but nothing like that materialized. Some children sang the national anthem, after which a bunch of balloons was released in the air.

Everyone clapped as they rose to the sky past a sprawling mango tree.

Then the participants were told to go to their respective rooms, with the seating arrangements being announced. Many of the students didn't bother to listen, trying to find their allocated rooms on their own.

Rasha found her allotted room too. Her seat was in a corner of a classroom on the first floor, next to a window. The view cheered her up at once. Visible was the lane below, with tin huts on either side. A young mother stood there with her baby. Rasha observed her with great attention. It was probably wrong to stare at a person without their knowledge, but Rasha proceeded to do just that with deep concentration.

Some people turned up to tell them some obvious things, accompanied by instructions on what they could and could not do. Then a bell rang somewhere and they were handed question papers and answer scripts.

Reading the questions carefully, Rasha was astonished. It was unbelievable—but she felt that she *would* be able to answer each of them correctly! She sat up and began to write.

Those who had set the questions had to be terribly clever, because the way they had composed the questions—which had to be solved one step at a time—made it impossible to answer without knowing the subject thoroughly. The last two questions were the most interesting. They provided some information at the beginning and then posed questions based on that information. Rasha had not been aware of how a supernova explodes—she had learnt about it from the question. Not only had she learnt the subject, but she had also answered a question about it! The other question was about proteins. The creation of proteins had been explained, followed by details about amino acids. And finally, several gene codes had been given from which the proteins had to be identified. Rasha marvelled at how interesting the question was!

Eventually the bell rang to signal the end of the exam. The invigilators began collecting the answer scripts. Rasha realized that she had forgotten to write her name and registration number. She wrote them down quickly, after which the name of the school had to be added. About to write 'Ahad Ali High School', Rasha paused. How could she write the name of a razakar on this answer script—the very razakar who had killed her nana? After some thought, Rasha put her pen down. She couldn't possibly write a razakar's name with her own hand! And besides, the name of the school couldn't be all that important—they could always get the details from her registration number if they needed to.

Emerging from the classroom, Rasha overheard two students walking in front of her.

One of them said, 'The questions made no sense!'

The other one replied, 'These people are ridiculous! They were trying to lecture us in the question paper, did you notice?'

'For heaven's sake, who has the time to read all this? Go on and ask your question quickly, we'll answer.'

'I'm not going to take part in these crazy things any more. Complete waste of time!'

'How many did you answer?'

'Five. I made some sense of three of them—I didn't understand the rest. You?'

'Six. But I'm in the same boat. The first three may be OK; I have no idea about the others.'

Rasha listened to them abuse the organizers of the Science Olympiad.

Strolling among those who had just taken the exam, Rasha tried to listen to their conversations. To her surprise, she discovered that most of them thought that they had performed badly. The questions, in their words, were 'lousy-fousy'.

The participants were then given lunch packets. Queuing up to collect hers, Rasha settled down in a corner to eat. Suddenly she felt upset. Everyone was chatting in pairs or groups. Many of the candidates had come with their parents, and others, with their teachers. All of them were together, eating and laughing. She alone was sitting by herself as she ate. Eating alone made you sad—there was something very depressing about it. Rasha went on eating sadly—biriyani soaked in oil, a boiled egg and a dry piece of chicken. Such a terrible meal.

There was a cultural programme in the evening—with well-known artistes singing, a dance performance, and, finally, a play. Rasha was watching a show like this after a long time—although she had been part of many such events herself when she attended school here. A small sigh emerged from her chest as she thought of those days. Almost immediately, Rasha wondered, with a frown, why people sighed when they felt sad. A sigh meant forcing all the air out of one's lungs—why did people do it only when they were wistful, but not at other times? Rasha was lost in thought.

In the evening they were taken back to the hostel in the bus. Not all the girls who had travelled in the morning were going back—there were just three of them in the bus. There were very few people who had neither friends nor relatives in all of Dhaka. The three of them in the bus were three such luckless people. Rasha glanced at the others from the corner of her eye—they were clearly from the villages, lacking the polish of Dhaka girls.

Rasha tried to strike up a conversation with the other two girls over dinner, but she discovered that they weren't very keen. There was something that they were apprehensive about.

The next morning there was a question-and-answer session. The experts were several old men, sitting on the stage. Rasha sighed when she set eyes on them. Old men always talked too much! She was sure that these people would also bore her to death. Still, Rasha waited with anticipation to find out what questions were asked and what answers the old men would give.

The first question was about why people become weightless in space. One of the experts on the stage answered in a roundabout way—no one understood him. This was how people answered when they didn't know something. One of the others appeared to disapprove of the answer. So he took the mic and proceeded to explain. This person was so enthusiastic, with so much to say, that he simply couldn't stop talking. When he finally finished, a girl asked why the acceleration of gravity at the centre of the earth was zero, when the formula that was taught suggested that it should be infinite.

Rasha sat up. She had worked out the answer on her own with great difficulty—she wanted to see if what the experts said matched her version. The people onstage were all great scientists, but they couldn't convey things clearly. They provided many explanations which nobody understood. The next question was about evolution, which a woman on the stage answered very well. The next person did not ask a question but delivered a short speech on the relationship between science and religion. One of the old men on the stage nodded, saying, 'The basis of religion is faith, and the basis of science is reason. These are distinct forms of knowledge. So science does not have to be explained with religion, and religion does not have to explained with science.'

The questioner was about to retort but the old man turned to someone else who had a question. This time the question was on the Big Bang. It was asked well, and answered beautifully too. Rasha had a question as well. The book that Jahanara Madam had given her talked of a strange form of science named quantum mechanics, which included an even more strange concept named wave function. This was what she wanted to ask about. There weren't too many people asking questions at the beginning. Had she put her hand up then, she would definitely have been given a chance. Now everyone had their hand up, so Rasha didn't try.

As the session was drawing to a close, a young woman came onstage with some papers, spoke to one of the old men, and then, taking the mic, announced, 'We're looking for a particular girl. She should come to our office at once. Her registration number is 2327. And her name is . . .' She glanced at the papers in her hand. Rasha was on her feet by then. It was her registration number, and, in fact, it was her name that was announced!

Rasha was worried. Why had she been singled out among thousands of students? There must be a problem, but what was it? But she must have got her answers right or they wouldn't be calling her, would they? Rasha felt both happy and afraid at the same time.

She followed the young woman, who said, 'My name is Mimi. I'm the coordinator here.'

'Why have you called me, Mimi Apu?' asked Rasha.

'I'm not sure. The controller of the examination has asked for you. Let's find out.'

Rasha followed Mimi up the stairs into a room on the first floor of the three-storied building. A bad-tempered man was sitting there.

He stared at Rasha over his glasses before rasping, 'So, you're that girl?'

Having no clue what he was talking about, Rasha was silent.

The man continued hoarsely, 'You've done very well in your exam—you've come first. But how can you be so careless?'

'*Careless?*' said Rasha.

'Yes. You've written your name and registration number, but not the name of your school!' The man showed Rasha her answer script. 'It says here that you have to write the name of your school, didn't you notice?'

Rasha was silent. The man said, 'The rules clearly say that your script will be cancelled in case of wrong or false or incomplete information. I could have cancelled your script if I had wanted to, girl. Do you understand?'

Rasha nodded to say that she understood.

The irritable man said, 'But how could I cancel the script of a little girl who has done so well in the exam? So I sent for you. Write down the name of your school now. Mustn't be so careless in future!'

Hesitating, Rasha said, 'I wasn't careless. I left out the name of my school deliberately.'

The bad-tempered man looked stern now. Looking at Rasha through narrowed eyes, he said, 'So you're not careless, you're a lawbreaker! You have no respect for rules and regulations—'

'No, it isn't that,' said Rasha quickly. 'Actually, my school's named after a razakar. I didn't feel like writing a razakar's name . . .'

The man glowered. Putting Rasha's script down on the desk, he sat up straight and glared at her. 'What did you say?'

'I said my school's named after a razakar, a name I don't feel like writing.'

'*A razakar?*'

'Yes.'

'How old are you?'

'Fourteen.'

'You're fourteen and you're getting into the politics of the freedom movement and razakars?'

'Not exactly the politics—'

Interrupting her, the man snarled, 'Listen to what I have to say! There's been enough politics in this country over the freedom movement and razakars. No more! Understand? Don't talk about things you've never seen for yourself!'

'But . . .'

Angrily the man said, 'I've heard a lot of empty talk. I'm not a young man. The more you say these pretentious things, the more you have to swallow them afterwards! Now it's up to you how you want to swallow them.'

Rasha guessed what he was trying to say. Still, she persisted, 'I don't understand what you're saying.'

'You understand perfectly. Here you are refusing to write a razakar's name. But you *will* write it, to claim your first prize. I'll cancel your script if you don't!'

Mimi was standing in silence all this while. Now she said a trifle impatiently, 'Let me find out the name of the school from her registration form, sir. I'll write it . . .'

The man screamed, 'NO! She must write it herself. She has to learn that spitting is easy, but swallowing your own spit is hard!'

Rasha felt as though there was a fire raging in her head. She couldn't think clearly. This was probably how her grandmother felt when she clutched her head with both her hands and muttered, 'Everything's upside down.'

'Write!' The furious man extended the answer script towards Rasha. 'Write down the name of your school named after the razakar!'

'I won't write it,' said Rasha.

The man was startled. 'What did you say?'

'I said I won't write the name of a razakar on my answer script.'

The man looked like he couldn't believe his ears. After some effort, he said, 'You won't write the name of your school?'

'No.'

'Then I'll cancel your script! You won't get the prize although you've scored the highest marks.'

'I know.'

'Still you won't write the name of your school?'

Rasha shook her head. 'No. I've spat, I won't swallow it.'

Grinding his teeth, the irritable man barked, 'You impertinent girl!' He glared at her ferociously for a while, and then said through gritted teeth, 'You don't know who I am. I wasn't bluffing, I really *will* cancel your script. Just watch . . .'

He took a red marker from his desk. Mimi ran up, trying to shield Rasha's script, saying plaintively, 'Please sir, please.

Don't cancel it! Give me five minutes, I'll find out the name of her school. Please!'

The man practically shoved Mimi aside, and then wrote on the answer script in large bold letters in English, 'CANCELLED'.

Tossing it away, he told Rasha, 'You may go now. If you ask me, I say go to hell if you so desire!'

Rasha left the room calmly, but tears began to flow from her eyes as she climbed down the stairs. She wouldn't cry, she vowed not to cry. But by the time she was downstairs, she was weeping uncontrollably. Hiding behind a pillar, Rasha tried her utmost to stop her tears but she just could not. Hiding her face in her hands, she sobbed; it would be very embarrassing if someone saw her.

Quietening down eventually, Rasha went back into the crowd. There was no point staying here any more. To tell the truth, her heart would break when the first prize would be awarded. How would she be able to bear it? Rasha realized that her anger was still seething within her. It required tremendous effort to calm herself down.

The headmaster had told her to stay there till the end of the prize distribution ceremony, after which he would take her back. So she would *have* to stay. What she could do, though, was to get out of here now and come back at the end of the ceremony. The programme was supposed to end at five in the evening.

Rasha walked out the gate. A busy street greeted her, with huge buses and trucks running on it. Rasha walked along the pavement, which was full of small shops selling all kinds of things. She came to an overbridge, under which she discovered an entire family living in a tiny coop. A baby was crawling. A child of four or five stood on the road, completely unafraid of the giant vehicles whizzing just past his nose. A man was selling a variety of books on the pavement. Rasha stopped to inspect them, but soon realized that she was staring blankly. She was so restless that nothing could calm her down. She felt like leaping in front of a moving bus.

'No, I won't do anything crazy,' Rasha told herself. 'What I've done is right. I'd decided not to write the razakar's name and I didn't. They can kill me but I won't write the name of the person who killed my grandfather! My nana was a freedom fighter, and I have fought for his honour. No one will know of this fight. Let *them* not know, but *I* will know.' Rasha kept muttering, 'I will know, I will know, I will know.'

She wandered around aimlessly. There were many people gathered at a bus stop, but it emptied out as soon as a bus arrived. Rasha sat there in silence. A madman was sitting on a bench across from her. He had a stubble, red eyes and yellowed teeth. The man smiled at Rasha as though he had known her for ages. Rasha turned her eyes away to gaze at the street.

Even after it was 5 p.m., Rasha waited a while before walking back to the venue. The prizes must have been distributed by now. She would not have to see the prize, that was rightfully hers, being given to someone else.

Opening the gate and walking in, Rasha was expecting to see an empty field. But to her surprise, she found the place full of people. As she walked on, she discovered someone about to make a speech. This must be the last speech, Rasha told herself, and went forward. There was a huge crowd and virtually nowhere to sit. Seeing an empty chair a little further ahead, she took it. Next to her was the bright-looking college girl she had met on the first day, the one who had suspected her of having had the problems solved by a grown-up. Rasha felt uncomfortable, but there was nothing she could do.

The girl asked, 'Did you come just now?'

'No, I came earlier and then went out for a bit.'

'OK.'

Hesitating, Rasha said, 'They must have given the prizes already.'

'No, not yet.'

Rasha was startled. '*Not yet?*'

'Any moment now. See, they're bringing them in.'

Rasha saw the medals being laid out on a table onstage. A young woman with a sheaf of papers was talking urgently to someone. Rasha felt her heart twisting. She wanted to jump up and run away, but she couldn't—it was too late now. She would have to watch the very scene that she had been trying to escape from. She had wandered all over and returned only to have to witness it. Why was the Lord so cruel? Rasha sat there, her head bowed.

The winners' names began to be announced, and each of the students shouted in joy and pranced to the stage. A man with salt-and-pepper hair, a stubble and a bushy moustache gave away the prizes. He must be a minister—Rasha had been told that a minister would distribute the prizes.

Twelve students were given the second runner-up prize, and another twelve, the runner-up award. Finally, six students won the championship prize. Most of the winners were boys, with only a handful of girls among them. Rasha discovered that it did not hurt as much as she had expected it to. Her senses seemed to have been dulled—she could feel nothing. She sat there in silence. As soon as the ceremony was formally declared over, she would get up and walk out. But the announcement for which she was waiting impatiently did not come.

The bright-looking girl next to her said, 'Something's gone wrong.'

Rasha lifted her head. 'What's gone wrong?'

'Look! A girl with some papers is screaming up there. They're trying to calm her down.'

Rasha looked at the stage to find the girl named Mimi talking animatedly, holding an answer script, while the others were trying to pacify her. Rasha realized at once what was going on. Mimi must have brought her answer script onstage, and was telling everyone that there had been grave injustice. Suddenly there were tears in Rasha's eyes.

The minister seemed annoyed at the commotion. He asked for Mimi to be sent to him. Mimi showed him the answer script, waving her arms and telling him something in great agitation. The minister looked at the script and then nodded. The old men were clustering around the minister, explaining something to him. He seemed to pay attention, and then shook his head.

The girl next to Rasha said, 'What do you think is happening?'

Rasha said, 'An answer script with the highest marks has been discovered, but the person hasn't been given a prize.'

'How do you know?'

'I don't. I'm just guessing.'

Suddenly the minister stood up and, taking the mic, he said, 'I want to make a small announcement. This Science Olympiad has been organized by well-known scientists and professors, and the answers have been evaluated according to their rules and regulations. They are all scholars and experts, far more knowledgeable than me, and the whole thing has been conducted as they had wanted it.'

Waving Rasha's answer script, he continued, 'Now, this particular answer script has just been given to me. It has been rejected because it did not follow the rules and regulations of the Olympiad. Which is fine—I have nothing to say about this. But what's very interesting is that this script belongs to a girl who has scored the highest marks. Higher than anyone else!'

There was a collective gasp of surprise from the audience.

The minister said, 'I respect the decision of the Science Olympiad committee. Let the rejected answer script remain rejected. But I want to offer this girl a personal prize. What do all of you think about that?'

'A prize! A prize!' shouted the thousand or so students and their parents in the audience.

'Then, Ma, come up on stage,' said the minister, calling out Rasha's name after reading it on the answer script.

The students, their parents and their teachers waited with bated breath to find out who the girl was.

Rasha sat still for a few moments. She had tears in her eyes, which she carefully wiped away with the back of her hand. Then she rose to her feet slowly. The girl next to her seemed to have a heart attack.

'It's you?' she screamed.

'Yes,' nodded Rasha.

The girl still couldn't believe it. *'Really?'* she asked again.

'Really.'

The girl emitted an ear-splitting shriek, as though it was she and not Rasha who had been called onstage. Leaping to her feet, she hugged Rasha and then half-carried her towards the stage, shouting all the time. An embarrassed Rasha tried to extricate herself, but the girl didn't let go till she had reached the foot of the stage and deposited her there, still shrieking at the top of her voice. Almost everyone present was on their feet for a closer look. Now they began to sit down again.

The minister led Rasha by the hand up to the stage. 'I want to give you a prize, Ma,' he said. 'Tell me what you want.'

The minister held the microphone in front of Rasha's face. She said, 'I have already got my prize. You calling me here is my prize.'

'Still, I want to give you something. Tell me.'

'Put your hand on my head and bless me.'

Those sitting in the front rows burst out in joy. The minister said, 'Of course I will, Ma.'

Rasha noticed an aged professor fidgeting behind the minister. Someone said loudly, 'There's been a misunderstanding, sir. We want to give her a special prize!'

Dismissing them with a wave of his hand, the minister said, 'No need. I think this girl will make great progress even without your prize.'

The aged professor said, 'But sir—'

Cutting him off with a gesture, the minister turned to Rasha. 'But Ma, there's something I don't understand. How can a girl who can solve such difficult problems at such a tender age forget to write the name of her school?'

'I didn't forget,' said Rasha.

'What is it then?'

'I left the name out deliberately.'

'Why?'

'Our school is named after a razakar. My nana was a freedom fighter, and this razakar killed him. I will die before I write his name.'

The minister gazed at Rasha with a strange look in his eyes. He had been talking into the microphone in his hand all this time. Now he put it down and, drawing Rasha close, whispered, 'Ma, I'm a freedom fighter too. Many of my friends were killed in '71. They were killed by razakars. I am an uneducated man, I didn't go to school. My friends were all talented boys—they would have been great men today if they'd lived!'

Patting Rasha on her head, the minister said, 'I'm giving you my word, Ma—I will change the name of your school within a week. I'll have the razakar's name removed and name it after a freedom fighter. After someone who was martyred somewhere in the vicinity of the school. All right?'

The minister asked Rasha this question in a way that suggested that everything depended on her answer.

'All right,' nodded Rasha. 'Thank you. Many thanks!' Then, though unsure of whether what she was doing was right, she hugged the minister and whispered, 'I'm not sad any more.'

Those sitting on the stage and those in the audience wanted to know what was going on. So the minister picked up the mic again and said, 'I've made a small promise to Ma here. I will change the name of her school. It will be named after a martyred freedom fighter. And my little Ma will then be able to proudly tell everyone the name of her school!'

As Rasha was getting off the stage, she was surrounded by television cameras. She noticed her headmaster pushing through the crowd to stand behind her.

One of the journalists asked, 'Are you upset at not getting the prize despite scoring the highest marks?'

Rasha shook her head. 'I'm not upset at all. My greatest prize is that my school will no longer bear the name of a razakar.'

No one had asked the headmaster a question but he added on his own, 'It's true that we have a problem with the name of our school, but it's a high-tech one. We have thirty computers! I am the headmaster, Kafiluddin, BEd.'

The journalists gathered around Rasha with more questions, which she tried to answer calmly. She felt nervous at times, but she noticed Jahanara Madam standing nearby, and Mimi next to her. Seeing them gave her courage, and she answered the questions with composure.

When the journalists left, Rasha ran up to Mimi to take her hand. 'Mimi Apu! How can I thank you!'

Mimi giggled. 'Shamshur Mian has been taught a lesson!'

'Who's Shamshur Mian?'

'The one who cancelled your script. He's the son of a razakar and a razakar himself. He'll lose his job for sure. The audacity!'

Jahanara Madam hugged Rasha. 'You're making me burst with pride, Rasha,' she said. 'Having even one or two students like you would mean that my life is fulfilled!'

The headmaster said, 'Rasha is actually a student of my school. I'm the headmaster! It's true that we have a problem with the name. But it's a good school! We have thirty computers. And three teachers with BSc degrees. My name is Kafiluddin, BEd!'

Jahanara Madam smiled. 'Your school *must* be excellent. How else could it have a student like Rasha?'

Ahad Ali, Razakar

The old signboard in front of the school was hauled down one day without any ceremony and a new one put in its place. In large letters it said, 'Shahid Rayhan High School.' Rayhan was a young man from the next village, a college student who had joined the war for freedom in 1971. He had returned after being trained, and then been killed in direct battle with the Pakistan Army, before he had turned twenty. The headmaster dug out a photograph—he looked like a boy, smiling shyly. The photograph was blurred because of enlargement. It had been framed and kept in the headmaster's office.

A smile appeared on Rasha's face every morning when she was still some distance away from school. The very thought that she would never have to utter the name of Razakar Ahad Ali filled her with satisfaction. What she wanted to know most of all was what he was doing now. She had heard that he was planning to file a case. Let him—Rasha was least bothered.

A few days later, as they were going home in the boat, Moti said, 'You probably need to be a bit careful, Rasha Bubu.'

'Careful! Why?' Rasha asked in surprise.

'Razakar Ahad Ali is very dangerous! He might try to harm you.'

'What harm can he do to me?'

'I don't know. But you should be careful.'

Moti was a boy of few words. So if he was warning Rasha, it had to be a serious matter.

'Has anything happened?' she asked.

'You could say so.'

'What is it?'

'We were on our way to school the other day, when a man drew me aside and asked, "Which of these girls is Rasha?"'

'What did you say?'

'I said that I don't know any Rasha.'

'Good!' said Jainab. 'There's no need to tell them anything.'

'I didn't, but someone else will.'

'That's true.'

Moti said, 'You mustn't go out alone, Rasha Bubu.'

'I hardly go out alone,' said Rasha. 'We're always in a group.'

'Yes, we have to stick together all the time from now on!' said Jainab.

They rowed their boat from the river into the lake, which was more or less deserted, with only a couple of fishermen in their boats in the distance. There wasn't a soul anywhere else. Rasha could hardly believe that the lake would dry up completely in winter, and that the water would be replaced by rice fields.

A few days later, as Rasha and her friends left school and walked towards their boat, she noticed that a man was following them. By the time they had left in their boat, he had been joined by three others, all of them staring at the children. No one knew what their intention was, but Rasha found the whole thing mysterious. Anxiety took hold of her heart.

It wasn't just outside that they were being followed by strangers. Some unknown men even entered school and began to peep into the classrooms. No one knew what they wanted. Rasha could neither tell anyone nor decide what she should do. She considered informing the headmaster, but what was the point? Perhaps she could let Salam Nana know, but Rasha was so busy with her exams that she didn't have the chance to meet him.

Rasha and her friends were returning from school in a group, and she was trying to check covertly whether anyone was following them. When she saw no one, she lowered her voice and said, 'You know what our problem is?'

'What?' said Jainab.

'We take the same route to and from school every day. So if anyone wants to intercept us, they know exactly what they have to do—they know where they need to lay a trap!'

'What must we do then?'

'We have to come to school from a different direction every day, and go home using different routes.'

'Don't worry, Rasha Bubu,' said Moti. 'I'll always be with you. No one will be able to do you any harm. They can't touch you as long as I'm alive.'

Rasha laughed. 'What will you do?'

'I'll kill them!'

'I'll be with you too, Rashapu,' said Jitu. 'I'll kill them too!'

Rasha giggled. 'With the two of you as my bodyguards, what do I have to worry about?'

They climbed into their boat, still chatting. After each of them had taken their seat, Moti used the punting pole to push the boat off. Then they used the oars to cross the river, taking the narrow canal near the bank to enter the lake. The water was dwindling here now, with the bare earth visible in places, covered in white *kash* flowers. The stalks swaying in the wind was a beautiful sight.

The lake was as deserted as on any other day, but there was a trawler in the distance, its engine audible despite the gap between them. Once they reached the lake, Rasha took the oar from Moti and sat down at the stern. She used it as a rudder, while Moti and Jitu rowed as if competing with each other. The boat was moving forward swiftly. When they had covered much of the way, they discovered the trawler heading across the lake towards them—it was quite close now. The roar of its engine had become deafening.

'Where's this trawler going?' asked Moti.

'Towards the river, probably,' said Jitu.

'Where's it coming from?'

'Who knows.'

Since there was no other vessel around, except the trawler, they stared at it with curiosity.

Suddenly its engine grew louder, and Rasha realized that it was racing directly towards them.

'Why is it coming towards us?' she asked, worried.

'I don't know,' said Jainab.

Moti picked up one of the punting poles. 'I don't like the signs. Its intentions aren't good.'

Rasha's heart thudded. What was the trawler trying to do? Now two persons appeared on the deck of the trawler. They had seen these two several times before—the men who had been following them like shadows.

'Don't be afraid, Rasha Bubu,' said Moti. 'I'm here.'

Rasha glanced at Moti. He was built like a reed. What could he do against two able-bodied men? 'Let's steer the boat towards the bank, near that thicket of kash flowers there.'

'All right!'

Rasha turned the boat. Moti and Jitu rowed with all their might so that they could put some distance between themselves and the trawler. But they discovered to their horror that it had changed direction too and was bearing down on them. There was no doubt about its intentions now!

It was upon them before they knew it, ramming their boat from the side, flinging all the occupants into the water.

The grotesque roar of the trawler, accompanied by the children's screams, made for a scene from hell.

The trawler did not stop, continuing to push the boat before it as it moved forward. Its occupants had no interest in those who had been thrown into the water. First Jainab and then Moti surfaced. Jitu swam up to them a little later. Two of the others had also come up to the surface by then, but not Rasha.

Jainab screamed in fear, 'Rasha! Rasha!'

There was no response. 'Rasha Bubu! Rasha Bubu!' Moti shouted at the top of his voice.

There was no answer this time either.

Floating in the water, they looked around in every direction but there was no sign of Rasha anywhere.

'Where's Rasha gone? *Where is she?*' Jainab said hoarsely.

At that precise moment, a man was holding Rasha down on the deck of the trawler. Wielding a knife used to slaughter cows, he was shouting over the noisy engine, 'Try anything funny and I'll slit your throat with this knife!'

Rasha did not try anything funny. The man's appearance, eyes and manner of speaking were all incredibly cruel. Rasha realized that he would have no trouble at all slaughtering a human being.

The man said, 'We should have killed you right now and buried you under the lake! But the boss wants to see you for himself first, that's why we're taking you to him. Don't you dare fool around!'

The whole thing became clear to Rasha. The boss had to be Ahad Ali, the razakar. That's whom these people were taking her to. When the trawler rammed the boat, she had been flung into the water just like the others. But before she could swim up to the surface, she had been pinioned by two arms as strong as steel. Rasha had tried to scream, but the sound had been drowned under the roar of the engine. Before she knew it, she was dragged out of the water brutally and pressed down on the deck. It had all happened in a flash.

Rasha was being held down with so much force that she felt her bones would break. She was having difficulty breathing but, at this moment, she couldn't even realize that she was in very big danger, for she had lost the power to think clearly. She felt as though she was in a daze, that this was a nightmare from which she would wake up any moment to find that none of this was happening.

But Rasha knew that this was no nightmare. She knew that all of this was real. She knew that survival would be a miracle.

Rasha had no idea how much time passed this way, but suddenly she heard the rumble of the engine fading. They had probably reached their destination. The trawler began to slow down and finally stopped.

Rasha heard the man holding her down tell someone, 'No need to go all the way up to the bank. Stop right here.'

'Right here?'

'Yes. If we go up to the bank, someone will see us and there'll be trouble!'

'All right, let me anchor the boat.'

Rasha sensed the trawler being stopped and anchored in midstream.

'When is the boss coming?' the other man asked.

The man holding down Rasha said, 'He isn't coming. We'll take her to him after dark.'

'What do we do with the hussy till then?'

'We'll tie her up. She's too frisky, you never know what tricks she'll be up to!'

Grabbing a handful of Rasha's hair, the man raised her to her feet. Brandishing the slaughtering knife near her face, he said, 'One false step and I'll kill you. Understand?'

Rasha did not speak. The man brought a dirty gamchha and gagged her so that she could not shout. Then he tied her hands tightly to the legs of a bench with another gamchha. Examining the knots, he made a sound of satisfaction and said, 'This should keep you quiet!'

Rasha had no choice but to sit quietly. Her body was turning numb with terror. She didn't know what to do. Closing her eyes, she prayed, 'Save me, Lord, save me. No one else can save me now, no one!'

Meanwhile, Jainab, Moti, Jitu and the others had gone straight to Salam Nana. Jainab was sobbing disconsolately, unable to speak coherently. Moti and Jitu were talking at the same time, making it impossible for Salam Nana to understand. Impatiently he said, 'One of you talk! Any one.'

Moti said, 'They've kidnapped Rasha Bubu.'

'Who's kidnapped her?' asked Salam Nana, shocked.

'A trawler came and rammed our boat; all of us fell into the water. Rasha Bubu wasn't there when we got out!'

'Could she have hurt herself and drowned?'

'She hasn't drowned!' Jitu said. 'We searched the entire lake—Rasha Apu isn't there. We found her bag, but not her.'

Moti said, 'The two men on the trawler used to follow us. They had asked us to point out Rasha Bubu to them.'

'Oh no!' exclaimed Salam Nana fearfully.

'What will happen to Rasha now?' Jainab sobbed.

Hurrying away, leaning on his crutch, Salam Nana said, 'We have to inform the police. The trawler must be located. Which way did it go?'

'Northward. Probably towards the Matakhali.'

'*The Matakhali!* Oh no!'

'Why is that bad?' Jainab asked through her tears.

'Ahad Ali lives on the bank of the Matakhali,' said Salam Nana.

Rasha tried several times to free her hands but without success. The knot was too tight to loosen in any way. She felt as though her blood circulation would stop. She moved her hand as much as she could, to keep the blood flowing. The dirty gamchha she had been gagged with made it difficult to breathe—at times she felt that she would choke. She was so thirsty that she could die for a drop of water.

The two men were sitting on the roof of the trawler, descending to the deck occasionally to check if everything was all right. Rasha could hear snatches of their conversation.

Suddenly she heard one of them say excitedly, 'Look! The boss is here himself.'

'Weren't we supposed to take the hussy to him after dark?' said the other one.

'Yes, we were. Let me find out what's going on.'

Soon Rasha heard a boat bump gently against the side of the trawler, followed by the sound of someone coming on board. One of the men said, 'You came yourself, *huzoor*? We were going to bring the hussy to you after dark!'

Rasha heard a deep voice say, 'No, I don't think we should delay things. I have been told that people who know her are suspecting that she's been brought here. There'll be trouble if the police find her here.'

'Don't we have our people in the police, huzoor?'

'That's how I found out. We have to finish things off quickly!'

'All right.'

'Where is she? Where's the hussy?'

'This way, huzoor. We've tied her to a bench.'

Rasha saw an old man coming towards her. He had a long white beard, and a round cap on his head. He was dressed in a kurta and lungi. This old man had to be Ahad Ali, the razakar. Rasha looked at him in wonder.

The bearded man leaned over her. 'Is this the hussy?'

'Ji, huzoor.'

'Remove that gamchha across her mouth, let me look at her.'

One of the men removed the gag. At last Rasha could take deep breaths. Her throat was parched. Gulping, she said, 'I want some water.'

'What did you say?' asked Ahad Ali.

'I said I want some water.'

Suddenly Ahad Ali began to rock forwards and backwards with laughter. The other two men looked at him in surprise, wondering what he was laughing about.

Ahad Ali said, 'Her grandfather had also said, "I want some water." And after all these years, even the granddaughter says, "I want some water!"'

Rasha looked at him and asked, 'Did you kill my nana?'

Suddenly everyone fell silent.

Rasha asked again, '*Did you kill him?*'

Ahad Ali's expression suddenly turned ferocious. Savagely he said, 'Yes, I killed him! And buried him under that coral tree there. So? What do you plan to do about it?'

Rasha's heart leapt into her mouth. This man just casually admitted to having killed her grandfather—he was not afraid to tell her this. This could mean only one thing. These people were going to kill her too—that's why they could tell her anything they wanted to. None of this would get out. Suddenly Rasha trembled with fear.

Licking her dry lips, she said, 'I want some water.'

The man next to Ahad Ali snarled at her, 'That's exactly what we've brought you here for. See that river there? You're going to drink *all* its water soon! With your mouth *and* your nose. And after you've drunk your fill, you'll sleep at the bottom of the river!'

The other man said, 'Your grandfather was India's pimp. A traitor! You'll meet him soon. The two of you can march together chanting "Jai Bangla!"'

'I want some water,' repeated Rasha.

The man was about to snarl at her again but Ahad Ali said, 'Give her some water. Last wish, fulfil it.'

'There's enough water in the river, huzoor. How much can she drink?'

'Enough! There's a water bottle in the boat, give her some.'

The man seemed positively annoyed as he went off to fetch the water. He came back a little later with a plastic bottle with some water at the bottom, tossing it at Rasha contemptuously.

'My hands have to be untied,' said Rasha.

The man threatened to slap her. 'What else do you want?'

Rasha said, 'How will I drink unless my hands are untied?'

'Untie her hands,' Ahad Ali instructed.

'What if she plays a trick?'

'With two able-bodied men like you here, what can this shrimp do?'

'I don't trust her! She's brazen.'

'All her brazenness will end soon. Untie her.'

Irked, the man untied Rasha's hands. They had turned blue. Rasha flexed her fingers. Her blood circulation began again, making them tingle.

As soon as Rasha tried to stand up, both men pounced on her. '*What?* What do you think you're doing?'

Rasha said, 'I want to sit on the bench properly.'

'*Indeed, your highness!*' one of them mocked her. 'Sit on the bench! Don't you dare get off the floor.'

Rasha gave up the attempt. Unscrewing the cap, she gulped the water down. Her breast felt like it was on fire, absorbing the water instantly. As she put the bottle down after draining the last drop, she had a brainwave.

A way to escape had occurred to her—a very difficult way, but still an opportunity! The empty one-litre plastic bottle had offered the chance. Her last chance. A chance to save her life. Rasha exhaled very carefully.

She finalized her plan in an instant. She would have to remove the bottom of the plastic bottle. Difficult, but not impossible—but she had to do it without raising suspicions. Rasha pretended to shake the bottle absent-mindedly, like people do when they're nervous. She had to keep talking too, to distract them. Not sure of what to talk about, Rasha asked, 'Why have you brought me here?'

Sitting down at one end of the bench, Ahad Ali said, 'You mean you don't know yet? I heard you on TV, I heard what you said.' He continued viciously, 'You're disgusted to even say my name? I'll teach you how to be disgusted! Not just you, I'll teach everyone who's ever known you.' Ahad Ali began to heap abuses on her in the foulest language. Had Rasha not heard it for herself, she would never have believed that an elderly man could say such obscene things.

Rasha pretended to be afraid. She tucked her feet under her, bit her nails. Then she folded the bottom of the bottle, tried to gnaw at it nervously and finally managed to slice a bit off the base. A sigh of relief issued from her. Whether she could survive or not depended on this plastic bottle. Now she inserted her finger into the hole she'd bitten off and tried to remove the base altogether. The sharp edge made her fingers bleed, but she kept working at it.

When Ahad Ali finally stopped with his expletives, Rasha asked, 'What will you do with me now?'

One of the men burst out laughing before Ahad Ali could answer. 'You hussy! Haven't you figured it out? Are you expecting us to make a bride of you? We're going to drown you! Got it?'

Rasha nodded to say that she had. She had almost loosened the base of the plastic bottle. Now she was preparing for the last move. As soon as these two men became a little careless, she would leap into the water. She had just the one chance. The last chance in her life. If she couldn't take it, no one would be able to save her.

Rasha muttered, 'Protect me, O Lord! I will never ask you for anything else in my life. Just help me a little now.'

Rasha looked at the two men. One of them was telling the other something; their vigilance had dropped. Rasha chose this very moment. Jumping to her feet with the bottle, she was about to leap like a cat into the water. The two men were flabbergasted, taking a few moments to register what had happened. They launched themselves at her, trying to stop her, but Rasha freed herself with a jerk and dove in.

She began to swim towards the bank. Taking one long, deep breath, Rasha sank under the surface, to swim underwater.

Ahad Ali rose to his feet with an obscenity. The men looked at one another, saying, 'This hussy is no end of trouble!'

'What are you standing there for?' said Ahad Ali. 'Catch her at once!'

'There's no need to hurry, huzoor,' said one of the men. 'How far can she go? We'll get her once she surfaces.'

The other man said, 'Does the girl think she can swim faster than me? Just let her surface!'

All of them stared in the direction in which Rasha had swum off. She would have to come up for air sooner or later, and then the two men would grab her.

They took off their shirts and hitched up their lungis, ready to dive in at a moment's notice. They stared at the water, waiting for Rasha to emerge.

But Rasha did not come up for air. The men watched in surprise as a minute passed, then two minutes, then five—but Rasha did not surface.

They glanced at one another. 'Where has she vanished?'

'Has she drowned?' Ahad Ali asked.

'She shouldn't. No one who knows how to swim can drown.'

'Then where is she?' Ahad Ali barked.

'That's what's unbelievable! No one can live without breathing. The hussy *has* to come up for air.'

They looked everywhere, but there was no sign of Rasha. She had not surfaced even once. The girl had disappeared, like a magic trick. Suddenly the men began to squirm uncomfortably.

Jumping into the water, Rasha swam towards the bank. When she had made a little progress, she raised her head, took a deep breath, and went underwater. Now she turned to the right, to swim along with the current, as quickly as possible, as far as possible. When she ran out of breath, she turned on her back and floated up so that the neck of the bottle rose above the surface. Her lungs were bursting for lack of oxygen, but she did not panic. Emptying the water that was in the bottle, she clamped the bottom on her mouth and took a single deep breath without surfacing. Then she dove in deep again, swimming underwater to get as far away as possible. When she ran out of breath, she used the same technique to take another deep breath. And so she continued.

Ahad Ali and his henchmen stood on the deck of the trawler scanning the water, but there was no sign of Rasha.

'What are you standing there like clowns for?' Ahad Ali bayed. 'Get into the water, find her!'

'But *where* has she gone?'

'Don't ask me! Find her.'

The two of them jumped in. They didn't know where to look but still they tried, without success. When they gave up after about an hour of searching, Ahad Ali noticed a police speedboat in the distance. He began to breathe raggedly—everything had gone wrong! He would be in deep trouble if the girl was alive. There would also be trouble if she had drowned, and her corpse floated up in a day or two. The plan had been to deposit the body in the waters of the lake so that no one could suspect him.

Salam Nana, Moti and Jitu were on the police speedboat too. The police disembarked and began a search, while Moti and Jitu stood on the bank, shouting, 'Rasha Apu! Rasha Apu! Where are you?' No one answered. They began to run along the bank, screaming, 'Rasha Apu! *Raaashaaa Aaaapuuuu!*'

Rasha was lying among the rushes, her body submerged and only her nose sticking out. Hearing Moti and Jitu, she sat up. When their voices became clearer, she came out of the water. Her body was caked with mud, her eyes were red from being underwater all this time, her face was drained of blood. Suddenly spotting her as they were running along, Moti and Jitu shouted with joy, raced down to the edge of the water and hugged her.

Moti held her tight, saying, 'Rasha Bubu! Rasha Bubu! You're alive? *You're alive?*'

Rasha had a bout of coughing. Then she said, 'Yes, Moti. The Lord saved me.'

'No one can touch you any more. No one. No one!' Moti hugged her close. Then he started weeping. Moti had never wept before—he hadn't known how to.

A stone-faced Ahad Ali was sitting in a chair in his yard. He was berating a police officer for suspecting him needlessly. At that moment, Moti and Jitu appeared, leading Rasha by her hands. Covered in mud, she was impossible to recognize, but still Ahad Ali recognized her and jumped as though he'd seen a ghost. His henchmen were standing on either side. They tried to run away but didn't get very far, for the policemen caught them.

Salam Nana hobbled towards Rasha, leaning on his crutch. Holding her, he said, 'Are you all right, Rasha?'

'No, Nana,' said Rasha. 'I have water in my nose and mouth.' Coughing, she said, 'I can't breathe, I think I'll die!'

'No, you won't die. You've survived—we won't let you die now.'

Rasha suddenly felt her legs buckle. She was about to fall when Salam Nana caught hold of her.

Rasha whispered, 'Let me tell you something now, in case I die.' Pointing to Ahad Ali, she said, 'This razakar here has told me that he killed my nana. He has buried the body under a coral tree.'

Rasha had another bout of coughing, and a stream of dirty, muddied water sputtered out from her nose and mouth. Suddenly she fainted, dropping into Salam Nana's arms.

'Speedboat, quick!' screamed Salam Nana. 'We have to take her to the hospital at once!'

The Last Word

A long time later.

The moon had risen in the winter sky, appearing hazy in the fog. There was a diffused glow from the moonlight. Anyone who listened closely could hear the drip of dewdrops from the leaves. Nani was about to go out with a lantern.

'Where are you off to, Nani?' Rasha asked.

Nani smiled shyly. 'Where can I possibly go? Just going to have a chat with your nana.'

'Can I come with you?' Rasha asked.

'*Come with me?* All right. You won't be afraid in the graveyard at night, will you?'

'No, Nani. I'm not afraid even if you are!'

Rasha looked at her grandmother from the corner of her eye. She was talking as though Nana really was waiting for her in his grave.

The remains of his body had indeed been found under a large coral tree behind Ahad Ali's house. Ahad Ali had identified the spot himself after being handcuffed. Rasha was present the day the body was dug out, although Salam Nana hadn't let her go near it.

'Don't go closer, shona,' he had told her affectionately.

'Why not, Nana?'

'Your nana was an incredibly handsome man. Let your imagination always picture him that way. Why should you upset yourself by seeing his skeleton instead?'

And so, Rasha hadn't taken a look at the remains of her grandfather's body. They had exhumed the corpse and put it in a coffin. Salam Nana had draped the red and green flag of Bangladesh around it. Thousands of people from the surrounding villages had borne the coffin to their village. Here, the final prayers were said and the coffin lowered into its grave after being wrapped in a white shroud.

Ever since then, Nani would come and sit by Nana's grave whenever she could. Rasha sensed that she was no longer as restless as she used to be, there was a certain peace within Nani now. She realized that Nani was waiting to join Nana.

Rasha and her grandmother were walking along the village path, their lanterns swinging, when a nocturnal bird flew overhead with a plaintive cry. Its call made the heart feel bereft.

Nani sighed, saying, 'Rasha.'

'Ji, Nani.'

'Have you received a letter from your mother?'

'No.' Rasha tried to laugh. 'That Mehtab—the peon—is lazy, Nani! He doesn't visit till there are a lot of letters to deliver.'

'I don't think your mother has much time to write.'

'That's true too.' Rasha paused before continuing, 'I think Ammu's angry with me, Nani. But what can I do—I no longer want to leave you and go to her.'

Nani didn't answer.

Rasha said, 'I may have gone if she'd been alone. But there's a man living with her whom I don't know. Apparently Ammu has persuaded him to accept my joining them. I mustn't be like other teenagers, I must behave—'

'I'm glad you didn't go,' said Nani. 'I think I'll die within a week if you leave.'

Rasha took her hand. 'Why would you die, Nani? You can't die now! Have you thought of what will happen to me if you die?'

Nani sighed again. 'No one is indispensable in this world, shona. Life goes on. Your life will go on too, even if I die.'

They arrived at the graveyard. Opening the iron gates, Rasha led Nani by the hand to Nana's grave. There was an intense fragrance of flowers. Wild flowers had blossomed somewhere. Putting the lantern on the gravestone, Nani sat down next to it, her legs stretched out. She gazed absently for some time, and then stroked the grave gently and lovingly. In the faint light of the lantern, Rasha saw two streams of tears trickling down her face. She had lost a loved one such a long time ago, but her sorrow did not seem to have faded yet.

Rasha looked on in wonder. Before her sat a human being. And that human being's sorrow.

There are three million human beings like her in this country. And three million sorrows. How had this land learnt to bear so much sadness?

Read More in Puffin

The Rhythm of Riddles
Three Byomkesh Bakshi Mysteries

Saradindu Bandyopadhyay
Translated by Arunava Sinha

Saradindu Bandyopadhyay's immortal detective, Byomkesh Bakshi, has enjoyed immense popularity for several decades. From being a household name in the Calcutta of 1930s when he was first created, to a popular face on TV in the 1990s—Byomkesh and his friend-cum-foil, Ajit, are perhaps the best-loved of India's literary detectives. These three mysteries are classic whodunnits that represent the best of detective fiction.

From a murder in a boarding house with too many suspects, to a mystery with a supernatural twist, and then busting a black marketeering ring in rural Bengal—the stories in this volume take Byomkesh to different locales on his quest for truth, and bring out the ingenuity and astuteness of this super sleuth.

Translated into English for the first time by award-winning translator Arunava Sinha, the breathless pace and thrilling plot of these action-packed adventures will win Byomkesh a new generation of admirers.

Read More in Puffin

Victory Song

Chitra Banerjee Divakaruni

Vande Mataram! The song of the freedom fighters is ringing in the countryside

The year is 1939. The freedom fighters will stop at nothing till they send the British back.

Twelve-year-old Neela arrives in Calcutta with a mission. Her father has been jailed for joining a protest march, and Neela has to rescue him before he is deported to the Andaman Islands. But can a little girl outwit the mighty British Empire?

Set in a dramatic period of India's history, this racy adventure, written by one of the finest Indian writers today, will keep you hooked till the last page.

'A well-paced, gripping story'—Booklist

'Brilliantly entertaining'—Voices from the Gaps

'A satisfying piece of historical fiction for pre-teens'—SAWNET (South Asian Women's NETwork)